JAN TURK PETRIE

The
Truth
in a
Lie

Jan Turk Petrie

ALSO BY JAN TURK PETRIE

Until the Ice Cracks
Vol 1 of The Eldísvík Trilogy

No God for a Warrior
Vol 2 of The Eldísvík Trilogy

Within Each Other's Shadow
Vol 3 of The Eldísvík Trilogy

Too Many Heroes

Towards the Vanishing Point

Running Behind Time

Contents

The Truth in a Lie

A Beginning of Sorts

London. August 2018

Today it hits me. Today is the day I'm leaving this house – a place I've lived for eleven of my forty-six years; almost a quarter of my lifetime. It's a beautiful sunny day outside but I'm going to be inside packing up my possessions, dismantling the home we've built together. There are many things I'll miss about this place. It especially pains me to be leaving behind my writing hut at the end of our long narrow garden – a space sufficiently removed from domesticity to enable me to produce a dozen novels out of thin air. I've been stuck on number thirteen for a while now.

My new place is not subdivided into small, intimate rooms like this house. Will I be able to write in the area I've earmarked in my new flat – my *loft-style apartment* as the agent insists on calling it? It's on the top storey of a former tea warehouse. The high ceilings made our footsteps echo when we looked around, but then it was empty. The only outside space is a balcony, which has just enough room for a table and a few chairs. Its saving grace is that it has a spectacular view of the river and beyond; that and the fact that I will be mortgage free at long last.

Perhaps I'll be able to write out there when it gets warmer. With less financial pressure, I might become a fair-weather novelist.

I pass Michael's study and the door is ajar. An invitation. His hall-of-fame photos have been packaged up and stacked against one wall. Despite the disarray, it's easy to picture him hunched over this antique mahogany desk, typing furiously to a deadline. Sensing me standing in the doorway, his head would flip round. 'Hi, Charlotte,' he'd say. 'Should be finished pretty soon.' With Michael soon could mean ten minutes or several hours. I learned not to take him at his word.

Downstairs, I find he's built a fortress of boxes to one side of the kitchen. From across the room, I'm drawn to a note he's left propped up against the Dualit toaster. An A4 sheet folded in half like a greetings card.

I don't know exactly what I expect it to say – maybe something touchingly corny along the lines of: *We'll always have Marrakesh…*

It reads,

Dear Charlotte,

I believe this toaster is mine and of course the coffee machine. The bread maker, vacuum cleaner and kettle are most definitely yours. You'll find I've clearly labelled the furniture and various sundry items I remember purchasing or brought with me – I thought it best to avoid any confusion.

Have a happy life,

Michael x

2

PS Please don't forget to hand your keys in to the agent when you've finished. I'll take mine round tomorrow once I'm all done here.

I note the formality of *Dear Charlotte* – I'm no longer Lottie. Impossible to miss the finality of *Have a happy life* and *I'm all done here*. That single kiss along with the happy life bit really gets to me. I screw up the note and drop it in the pedal bin, which he's welcome to. 'Four bloody years and that's all you have to say.'

'Who are you talking to?' Kate demands. She's out of breath and frowning; a pack of flattened boxes is wedged under one arm. The faded t-shirt she's wearing is from the concert she went to as a birthday treat when she was fourteen; the same band she recently described as *shit*.

As a bracelet she's sporting an oversized roll of tape marked FRAGILE. I take it and the marker pens from her. There's a loud whack when she drops the boxes onto floor; though I watch it happen, it still makes me jump.

Stepping over them, Kate asks, 'Who were you swearing at just now?' She looks around the room as if expecting someone to be lurking in a corner.

'It's nothing,' I tell her.

I eye up the shiny bean-to-cup coffee machine – Michael's pride and joy. How often have I witnessed him demonstrating the whole barista thing to our friends? Such an indulgence; I know for a fact it cost him the best part of two grand. Shouldn't that have told me something about the man? I mean, who would spend that sort of money on a kitchen gadget when they've just arrived back from reporting on a famine?

I turn to Kate, clap my hands and say, 'Let's have a coffee before we get stuck in.' Sabotage, though tempting, would be petty. Am I above pettiness?

She says, 'I'd rather have a herbal tea.' Her diet's undergone a radical change in the year since she left home. For Kate, student life is most definitely not about sex, drugs and rock 'n' roll; exorbitant tuition fees have put paid to the hedonism of the past – my past.

Bingo! There's a sealed pack of the special beans he likes still in the cupboard. When I break the seal, the distinctive earthy smell escapes. I measure out an appropriate amount and, whilst the beans grind away, locate my favourite handmade mug. Kate is saying something to me, but any conversation is impossible over the machine's noise. Always has been.

I have to admit the resulting coffee is seriously delicious. Should I buy one of these for my new flat? Not a monster like this one – something more proportionate and definitely cheaper.

Opposite me, Kate is sipping her pale-as-anything tea. She looks distracted, downcast. Though this move has been months in the making, it hasn't necessarily made it any easier on her. I touch her hand. 'Is everything alright?'

'It's nothing. I mean, I was just thinking…'

I wait.

'I know he was away an awful lot,' she says. 'But still it's going to be odd, you know, not having Michael around anymore.'

'Of course it will be.' I squeeze her hand. 'It's okay to miss him. He might not be your father but the two of you always seemed to get along pretty well.'

'That's the thing,' she says. 'I thought we were, well, friends – in a way. I figured that he'd want to stay in touch after the two of you split, except –'

'Except what?'

'Except whenever I've phoned him, he's always too busy to talk.'

It's as much as I can do not to curse the man out loud. Instead I say, 'I'm sure he's just a bit preoccupied – you know how he gets when he's working on something.' This at least is true; obsessive doesn't begin to cover it.

'Maybe.' She looks unconvinced.

When she finally meets my gaze, I smile and sweep the dark hair that's fallen across her face behind her ear. Her skin is so delicate and unblemished – a blank canvas if you didn't know any better.

She undoes the elastic band holding her ponytail and pulls her hair back together hand over hand with a ferocity that ought to hurt. 'Anyway,' she says doubling up the elastic, 'hadn't we better get cracking before the removal men arrive?'

I glance at my watch. 'Yep, better get a move on – excuse the pun.'

Her smile is genuine. 'That was awful, even for you.'

I drain my coffee, rinse the mug under the tap and dry it. Tearing off a piece of bubble-wrap, I secure it with the FRAGILE tape, do my best to protect it from any damage.

By rights I should clean his precious coffee machine. But then, by rights Michael Burrows should be a better human being.

We drive over to the new flat ahead of the vans, my ancient Fiat loaded high with our suitcases and the bits and pieces I thought we might need right away. I'm driving so it's Kate who takes the call from the solicitor confirming that everything has simultaneously completed. 'He says you're now the legal owner,' she relays. 'The concierge has been told to release the keys to you.'

I say, 'That's a relief,' because it is.

Michael has been given special permission to move his things out tomorrow morning but from this moment on I have no right to ever go back… home.

'It's so weird we now have a *concierge*,' Kate says. I'm pleased she used the word *we*. At the traffic lights I snatch a glance in her direction but she's looking straight ahead. From her profile, I'd say she's not especially happy, disappointed perhaps there'd been no last-minute reprieve.

My car doesn't have sat nav so we use my phone to guide us there. Hazard lights flashing, I park in the narrow cobbled street outside. With its weathered brick façade, the old warehouse building looks solid and dependable; the sort of place you might find shelter in a zombie apocalypse.

The concierge is based in the adjoining block – the one with the much fancier apartments. From behind a counter in the impressive lobby she hands out a professional smile along with my keys then welcomes me to the complex as if this were a hotel instead of my new home.

Weighed down with a bizarre assortment of our possessions, Kate and I squeeze into the lift. I unlock the door and dump my laptop and the other stuff in the kitchen area.

Looking around, I find it hard to take in the fact that this empty, elegant shell is where we're going to be living from now on. There are no curtains at the patio doors, no rugs to relieve the hardness of the flooring. Once again I fancy I can smell tea – that the fabric of the building has been steeped in its essence.

'That one is your room.' I point to the largest of the two.

Kate frowns. 'How come I get the biggest one? I mean, it's not like I'm going to be here most of the time anyway.'

'Still, I want you to see this as your home too,' I tell her. Not for the first time I wonder if this has all been a colossal mistake. I open the bedroom door to tempt her inside. 'This one has more room for a desk. I thought I'd buy a daybed which should fit under the window.' I stand in the space I think it could go in and hold out my arms to illustrate my point. 'It'll be somewhere to sit when you want some privacy and you can use it as a bed when your friends come to stay.' One eyebrow raised, she gives me a look that suggests this is an unlikely scenario.

'We could even put a TV on the wall over there,' I say.

'A telly in the bedroom – isn't that against the rules?'

'When you were little, yes.'

She shrugs. 'No need anyway, I can just use my laptop.'

Movement in my peripheral vision draws my attention down to the street below where the black hat of a traffic warden is circling around my car. It must be clear that these are exceptional circumstances; the kettle pressed up against the back window would suggest the owner is in the process of moving in.

I rush downstairs and do my best to reassure the woman that, once everything is unpacked, I'll move the car to its designated subterranean parking space. Given how seldom I use it, I doubt my poor old Fiat will be seeing the light of day for some time.

Failings

September 2018

It's taken a while to get things straight but I'm pleased with the way the flat is now looking. After a lot of rearranging, our furniture seems more at home than it did at first. I've seen off the last of the boxes and all the books are sitting on shelves – admittedly not in any logical order but eventually they will be.

The new rug offers comfort to my bare feet. Mug of tea in hand, I'm about to open the balcony doors when I see the rubber plant my friend Karen gave me as a housewarming present. Last week I'd noticed there were brown edges to several of its leaves and so I'd watered it and moved it further into the light. The leaves are now lying wizened on the floor. From the state of the poor thing, I'd say the rest of its foliage is about to drop off. I remember a reformed character in some film being given a houseplant to tend as the first step in learning how to nurture other living things. Judged by the same criteria, I must have a long way to go before I'm ready for a new relationship.

Kate emerges from her room looking miserable. I'm aware of the significance of today's date and this is a bad sign. She lingers in the doorway. I can see her eyes are bloodshot; it's obvious she's been crying.

She finally looks at me and says, 'Just got my results. I screwed up – royally, as Dad would say.'

My smile tries too hard. 'Are you sure it's that bad?'

I've said the wrong thing. 'Course I'm bloody sure,' she snaps. 'All that work and I still managed to get below the pass mark in three of them.'

I take a step towards her, tentatively put an arm around her shoulder. It's a relief when instead of shrugging me off, she leans her head against me. 'Maybe I'm just thick,' she says sniffing.

'Of course you're not.' I hug her closer. 'Listen, these things happen, Kate – Exams can be tricky – it's a lot of pressure. And, you know, people have their off days–'

'Yeah well, I'm having an off *year*.'

Guilt overwhelms me; after all it was my decision to sell her childhood home and uproot her. 'The move can't have helped,' I say and she doesn't deny it. She'd also broken up with her boyfriend not long before the exams but I think it best not to bring him into the equation.

As a child Katie was chubby, a robust little thing, but now she feels so slight and insubstantial; I daren't squeeze her too hard. Stroking the back of her head I say, 'I'm sure they'll let you sit them again.'

'Yeah I know.' She pulls away. 'But that's not the point, is it? I mean, maybe I'm not up to it.' She kicks the doorframe. 'P'raps I'm just too fucking stupid.'

'Don't talk like that.' I grab her arm, shake it gently. 'Your coursework marks have been fine – good in fact. This is just a blip; you'll get over it. It'll work out okay in the end, you'll see.'

'You can't possibly know that,' she says. Her mobile rings. She looks at the screen and groans. 'God, it's Becky.' She throws the phone onto the kitchen table – it lands harder than can be good for it. 'I can't face her fucking pity.' She subsides into a chair and, face down, rests her head on her arms.

In her place I would crack open the vodka but not Kate. Without asking, I make her a herbal tea and put it in front of her. Could be the smell of lemongrass and ginger that makes her lift her head. Sitting up, she cups it in her hands and simply stares at the floor.

Out of her line of sight, I send Duncan a text giving him the bad news. Then I make a start on our supper – the vegan shepherd's pie she's especially fond of; under the circumstances it's hard not to treat her like I might if she were ill.

Chopping garlic, I hear her talking on the phone. From snatches of conversation I can tell it's her father. Five minutes of yeahs and nos and then finally I hear her laugh. It sounds genuine.

I carry on chopping, distracting myself. She's gone quiet. After a few mmms she starts to giggle. 'Really?' Is she talking to Duncan or one of the boys?

Her call finished, she walks over to the kitchen area. The island lies between us. She asks, 'Did Dad ever tell you how he totally screwed up his A-level exams the first time?'

Though I know this, I play along. 'Did he really?'

'Yeah, he had to retake them – that's the reason he took a

gap year. After the retakes, he went travelling. He says, looking back, it was the best thing that could have happened to him; that at the time he didn't imagine he'd end up as a professor.'

'I don't suppose he did,' I say. 'And you know I expect there'll be other people on your course in the same boat.'

She looks unconvinced. 'Maybe.'

Spinning round on one foot she says, 'This place is very different to Dad's.' The heat from the simmering vegetables rises into my face. 'It's so quiet here; everything's so orderly with just the two of us. We haven't even got a pet.'

'They're not allowed in the lease,' I tell her.

'Exactly. Here, they've outlawed barking, even mewing, like making a noise is some sort of crime. At Dad and Sarah's there's always something going on. I mean Charlie's totally wired half the time. Ben was the same until he discovered gaming. And Ripley's always running about barking because Charlie won't throw his stick for him.'

I add chopped tomatoes to the mix.

'It's more fun there.'

'Is it?'

'Yeah, although Dad's always saying the place is a madhouse and he can't hear himself think. He tries to calm everybody down. Sarah just yells at them. She's always saying she never gets a minute to herself.'

I decide not to comment. I would never openly judge my ex-husband's wife but the woman holds down a job with a six-figure salary, so it's hard not to take this without a very large pinch of salt. I say, 'Young children can certainly be demanding.'

Leaning across, Kate dips a teaspoon into my saucepan, scoops up some of the mixture and blows on it. Wafting a hand to help it to cool, she asks, 'Is that why you only had me?'

'Not exactly.' I add the lentils. Now is not the time to elaborate.

She shrugs and dips the spoon in again. 'Have you got any oregano?'

I find the dried stuff and shake some in. 'Right,' I say, 'would you rather have sweet potato mash or ordinary mash?'

Without answering, she takes out her phone and strolls towards her bedroom and the privacy she needs. Over her shoulder she says, 'Sweet potatoes sound great. No butter though.'

Kate wasn't quite two when we decided to try for another baby. Before she was born, Mum had given us a book of potential names. When I got pregnant the second time, Duncan would bring it out at bedtime and suggest stupid ones. He'd try to wind me up by putting his hand on my expanding stomach and saying things like, 'How's wee Hamish Maloo today?' or 'I think I felt little Tinsel-Tigermoth move.'

With Kate I'd felt permanently sick through most of it, but with this pregnancy I didn't. I thought it meant my body had cracked the baby thing.

It was high summer – a lovely bright day as I recall. I was in the supermarket with Katie in the trolley's child seat. I felt a sharp pain in my groin. I did my best to ignore it. The next one was stronger and more worrying. When I lifted Kate down from the seat, I felt a dragging sensation low down. In the toilet cubicle, I found blood on the tissue. Not much, just a smear.

I'd left my half-filled trolley outside and I wondered if I should carry on and finish the shopping before going home. I stood there for a few minutes before my legs turned to jelly. I became hot and breathless and I thought perhaps I ought to sit down and maybe ask someone for a glass of water. Should I buy some sanitary towels? Call Duncan? Or should I simply get in the car and drive to the nearest hospital?

Unconcerned, Kate was chewing a toy dinosaur. Holding her hand tightly, I went back into the main shopping area, and looked around hoping there might be someone who could help me. There were no obvious candidates; no one dressed as a nurse or with a stethoscope hanging from their neck. Amongst my fellow shoppers I couldn't spot any wise old women who might advise me. Everyone was too busy to notice.

In the end I went outside. Glad of the fresh air, I strapped Katie in her car seat before driving the short distance home. I did all this as if on autopilot; I felt detached, like it was happening to someone else.

I don't recall the journey or getting out of the car. I remember I put Katie down in her playpen – something my mum had given me, which we used mainly to store toys. I cleared most of them out but left a few to distract her.

When I went to the toilet, there was more blood but I felt no pain. Katie was already screaming with indignation. I found her sobbing and clinging to the side rails, but I left her there while I called the surgery.

The receptionist informed me there were no doctors in the building – that they'd all finished their morning shifts. 'Is it an emergency?'

'I'm not sure,' I said. 'I think it might be.'

'Is there something wrong with your baby?' she demanded. 'I can hear it screaming.'

'I don't know. I can't think,' I said and hung up.

I checked my watch. It was lunchtime – Duncan might be in the refectory. 'He's off-site this afternoon with the rest of the department,' the secretary reminded me.

I felt something running out of me so I went back to the toilet and discovered more blood – darker blood. I found a sanitary pad.

Katie was bashing her toys together. She was calmer; her crying had become a snivel. I sat back on the sofa and phoned the surgery. 'Hi, this is Charlotte Warrington again; I think it's probably an emergency after all. I seem to be having a miscarriage.'

This time the woman went off to find a nurse.

An older voice asked, 'Which trimester are you in, Mrs Warrington?'

It was hard to think, 'Second.' I was shivering.

'And you're Doctor Robert's patient?'

'Yes, although I've seen more of the female doctor; Doctor Patel.'

'But you're registered with Doctor Roberts?'

I wanted to ask what the fuck it mattered but I just said, 'Yes.'

'And is anyone else there with you?'

Her curious eyes were right on me. 'Yes, Katie, my daughter. But she can't help me, she's only a toddler.'

'Okay, I want you to stay calm, Mrs Warrington. Sit yourself down. What's your first name?'

'Charlotte.'

'Okay, Charlotte, can you confirm you're currently at your home address?' She read it out.

'Yes, that's correct.'

'Good. Listen carefully; someone will be there with you very soon. It's important that they can gain access to your home.'

Before the ambulance arrived, I unlocked the front door and left it ajar. It seemed a rash, imprudent thing to do.

It was clear something was about to happen. Bent double with pain, I hobbled into the bathroom and collapsed on the floor. My overriding concern was that I didn't want Katie to witness any of it. Though she was only a toddler at the time, those sorts of things can stay with you, screw you up for years afterwards.

I remember the relief I felt when the paramedic arrived; naively I imagined a miracle might still be possible. As frightened as I was, I hadn't envisaged that the events of that day would change the course of my life.

An Uninvited Visitor

At first I don't hear it but then the swell of the orchestra begins to subside and the entry-phone buzzer takes over. 'It's me,' his voice tells me. 'I promised to pick up a book Kate needs for revision. I'm seeing her at the weekend.'

Though I'm irritated that he hadn't thought to ring ahead, I say 'Ah yes. She sent me a text about it. Come on up.'

I watch for the top of Duncan's head to appear. There's a scrabbling noise on the stairs beside him; I'm more than a little surprised that he's brought his dog along.

I show him into my living-come-everything room. His raincoat looks soaked through at the shoulders. 'So this is your new place,' he says looking past me. 'Wow, what an impressive space. I like the bare brick over there. Great view; you can see the boats on the river.' Meeting my gaze at last, he smiles. 'I expect you've already noticed all that.' His tanned skin looks unnatural in this cloudy London light. Perhaps he's just returned from a trip; they've probably been somewhere fashionable in the Caribbean or staying with Sarah's family in California.

Several times his hand rakes the damp hair away from his face in a nervous way. 'I bet you never tire of watching the world from this eyrie of yours.' Still handsome, that's for sure. The sun has bleached his hair a shade lighter on top. I spot some white at his temples and threaded through his stubbly beard. It's probably the weather that's made his cheeks redden.

'You're right,' I say. 'I find it endlessly fascinating.' I'm wearing my poker face, determined not to show how pleased I am to see him.

The tail of the shaggy brute by his side begins to beat the floor, anticipating attention. 'This must be Ripley.' I stroke the dog's damp ears and they're impossibly soft. 'I've heard about some of his escapades from Kate.'

'I bet. The two of them have always been besotted with each other. When he was a puppy, she used to encourage him to sleep on her bed. As you can see, he's a bit too big for that now. Doesn't stop him trying to sneak in there when she's staying with us, though.

'You're looking well,' Duncan says taking a step towards me. 'Your hair's different.'

'It's the highlights,' I tell him. 'Brown is just boring; I thought it might brighten it up – brighten me up, I suppose.'

'Well it suits you,' he says. This close, he's too close. I have to turn my head to be certain his kiss glances off onto my cheek; the contact with his stubble leaves my skin tingling. Ripley takes this as his cue and starts wrapping himself around my legs, dampening my jeans. The distinctive smell of wet dog is taking over my apartment.

I disentangle myself from both of them and walk over to the kitchen's island to put a solid block between us. The music has entered a lighter passage – easy harmonies like a rom-com soundtrack.

I blip the remote to silence it. 'How's academia?' I ask.

He shrugs. 'Pretty much the same as always. Though since I'm now head of department, I have to show my face more often than I used to.'

'Congratulations on your elevation.' I didn't mean it to sound so sarcastic. Remembering my manners, I say, 'Can I get you something? Cup of tea? Coffee? Something a bit stronger?'

'Coffee would be great thanks.' He takes off his waterproof and drapes it over the back of a chair where it starts to drip onto the floor.

I jump when he snaps his fingers and points to the rug. With a disappointed sigh, the dog folds his long legs and sits down. I watch the animal's red-rimmed eyes move from him to me before giving another long sigh; his awkward limbs take up a surprising amount of space.

The noise from my new coffee machine makes it impossible to talk. I would offer Duncan a biscuit if I had any. He used to have a sweet tooth but maybe that's changed. 'I'll go get that book,' I say.

In the privacy of the spare room, I check my appearance in the mirror. I brush my hair into place and borrow some of Kate's mascara. Once I've found the right book, I take a steadying breath and open the door.

The racket from the machine has subsided. Duncan is still

on his feet, looking restless. I place the book on the table in front of him. From the floor, Ripley is eyeing me up. I can't resist the animal's forlorn expression; when I go over to stroke his narrow muzzle, he raises his head to lick the coffee powder from my hand. 'He's very well behaved,' I say.

'I can't take any credit for that, quite the opposite,' Duncan says. 'When he was a puppy, he was pretty wild. Kate was his partner in crime. Ever the pragmatist, Sarah sent him off to some kind of boot camp for naughty dogs. It did the trick – he came back fully trained and obedient.' Do I detect a hint of regret in his voice? Head on one side, he regards the dog. 'Although one or two bad habits have snuck back in since then, haven't they, Rip?'

'I'm sure you wouldn't want him to be too perfect – to lose all his spark.'

'Quite,' he says.

'How is Sarah?'

'She's fine.' Glancing away, he strolls around surveying my paintings and books. It's odd to see him here – to have him pacing around in my private space. He walks over to my desk and stops in front of it. 'Looks like you've got another book on the go. What's this one about?' He bends to read the manuscript's title page: 'By Whose Hand?'

'A working title – or more accurately a not-working title.' I hold up both hands like it's not important. 'It's nothing – a project I've struggled with and decided to abandon. Needless to say my publishers aren't overjoyed about my change of heart.'

'But you've printed the whole thing out.' He picks up the

manuscript, weighs it in his hand. 'Doesn't look like nothing to me.'

'Okay, it's something; but it's not right. Fatally flawed, as it were.' I pull a pained face. 'Even more than the others.'

'Still your own harshest critic,' he says, flicking through it.

'Please don't.' I almost snatch the thing out of his hands. I put it down again, out of his reach.

He's taken aback, so much so that I feel the need to explain. 'It's based on a true story,' I say, 'though I'm not sure whether there can ever be such a thing. What do we mean when we talk about *the truth*? Always such a hard thing to pin down.'

I can't decipher the expression on his face. My eyes are drawn to the faded scar on his cheek – how it stops just short of his mouth. It definitely wasn't there when we were together. Must have been a pretty deep cut to leave such a mark. 'Surely you can find out the truth,' he says. 'If you put together all the known facts.'

'But how do you find out *all the facts*? I mean aren't there an infinite number to choose from?' I can feel my face begin to redden because this must sound like the lead up to a deeper conversation about the truth in our own particular history.

Determined not to go there, I slip into lecture mode. 'As a writer, one can't avoid choosing which particular *facts* to give more credence to. Besides that, only certain things get recorded or are remembered. Everything is biased, the recorder, the witnesses; even the reader – all are inevitably partisan.'

Remembering too much for my own good, I go over to pour the coffee. I put both cups on the low table and sit down on the sofa, plumping up the cushions I'd sprawled out on watching a late-night movie.

He comes to stand before me, the spotlights almost transforming his hair into a halo. Narrowing his eyes, he says, 'Why abandon the whole project when you've put so much effort into it? There must be something you can salvage.'

I've been over all this with Jenny, my agent. 'It's not possible,' I tell him. 'I don't usually base my novels on true stories so I was naïve when I started. I thought that if I did enough research, I could get to the truth of what happened. But I can't begin to tell any kind of story without making things up – too many things.'

He finally sits down in the chair opposite. Fingers fiddling with a loose thread on the arm, he says, 'I suppose we can't know everything about other people's lives. Perhaps we shouldn't even try. Better to leave a few mysteries.' He clears his throat. 'Besides, each of us makes up our own narrative – our own version of what went on.'

I'm about to say something back but bite my tongue. The two of us fall silent. I listen to Ripley's rising snores.

Finally, Duncan nods towards my desk. 'So this abandoned book of yours – what was it about?' Is he just making conversation or does it really bother him?

I ask him if he remembers the Serena Bianci story. 'It was in all the newspapers at the time,' I tell him.

'Oh yeah – I remember reading about it.' He shakes his head. 'Awful business.'

'Well, I wanted to tell Serena's side of the story – to restore her voice in some way. But I was wrong about that. I'd written that little lot before a new source led me to discover several things that didn't fit my version of events.'

'Like what?'

'It'll probably sound stupid to you.'

He leans forward and says, 'Why don't you try me?'

'Well, as an example, there was her wedding outfit. I came across a full-length photo clearly taken on the day. I'd previously only seen the head and shoulders shot used by the newspapers so I'd imagined the rest. I described her outfit as demure, understated. But that was literally only half of the picture.'

He puts his cup down. 'So what was the rest of it like?'

That awful feeling comes back just thinking about it. 'The skirt was a big surprise – it was anything but plain; it had these huge multi-coloured flowers all over. What my mum would call a loud pattern.'

'Isn't all that just irrelevant detail?'

'A woman's wedding outfit tells you a lot about her. It made me realise it was *my* Serena I'd been writing about; not the real one.' I throw up my hands. 'When I saw that damned skirt, I thought – if I could get something like that so wrong, how could I know anything for certain? And I was right – the more I learned, the further away my version of events proved to be.'

I'm embarrassingly close to tears. Duncan notices. His voice is gentler when he says, 'It must be upsetting to have wasted all that time on something you then have to abandon.' I pick up the subtext. He gets up and comes to sit beside me. In sympathy, his dog moves across to rest his sleepy head on my knee.

This close I can smell the fabric conditioner on his jumper. I resist the urge to lean my head against his chest. Instead, I wipe my eyes with the heel of my hand, no doubt smearing Kate's mascara in the process. 'It coincided … I mean I was trying to write it at a difficult time.' I'm pretty sure Kate must have filled him in on the fine details of my split with Michael. 'I think I went a bit off the rails for a while.'

He sighs. 'Happens to the best of us.'

'And you know at my age you'd think I'd be able to stay professionally detached but I allowed the whole Serena thing to possess me. Was she guilty or innocent? I became obsessed with knowing the truth. I get to play God in my stories – I control my characters' lives, their destinies. It's probably not very healthy; you can get used to being omniscient.'

Ripley groans on my behalf.

'Listen, Goddess.' His arm comes round my shoulder – a light hesitant touch. 'It's only natural to be upset. I mean, after all the work you put into these, um, things.' He squeezes my upper arm and I breathe in his aftershave – subtle spicy notes that do nothing for my resolve.

To break the spell I pick up my coffee. When I take a sip it's too hot and burns my mouth. Putting my cup down, I look into his dog's knowing eyes and wonder why he's brought him here today.

'What do our clothes really say about us?' he says. 'I mean, look at my jeans – I don't even remember where I bought them. The woman's choice of skirt– does it really matter? Maybe you're making a mountain out of the proverbial molehill?'

'It's not that simple,' I tell him.

'Couldn't you just rewrite some of it?'

'The truth is, I really haven't the heart for it – not now. Not ever.'

'Then why not shred the bloody thing? Or better still set fire to it. Exorcise those lingering demons and move on.'

Before I can answer, the landline phone rings. To distinguish it from my mobile, I set its ringtone to the classic, echoing *burr-burr*. A sound straight out of a black and white movie – a summons you ignore at your peril.

Duncan frowns. His expression says, *aren't you going to answer that?*

Hardly anyone rings me on my home phone these days. As I lift the handset, I steel myself in case this might be bad news.

Heading North

My windscreen's awash with the dirt-laden spray coming off the lorries. Big bullies – they jostled us this way and that. Living in the capital, I rarely drive and haven't got round to replacing my ancient Fiat; this is its longest trip in six months.

A mix of snow and rain is falling; the wipers smear it all to one side in grating arcs leaving me only two small wedge-shapes to peer through. How would I describe the stuff that's hitting the glass? Slew? Slain?

I exit the motorway and the roads get narrower. It's a strain having to squint through two intersecting triangles. Though it's daylight, the oncoming cars have their lights on. It would be easy to miss the turn-off. I have to avert my eyes from the stream of traffic and follow the edges of the road; the bare-limbed trees lining up one after the other.

When I get to the house it plays that shrinking trick on me once again. Tiny ice particles hit my face as soon as I leave the shelter of the car. The wind messes with my hair while my hands struggle to sort out the keys.

Once inside, I try not to breathe in that empty smell. The

house is bitterly cold. If Mum was here, I'd take my shoes off; but she's not. My wet footprints trail across the tiles to the carpeted front room. To deter burglars, she's left the place in a quandary – lit by a couple of lamps while the curtains are only half-pulled. I tug them back to look out on the town. The gaps that used to give a view of the moor have all been neatly filled up. An overgrown shrub keeps whipping the glass like it's trying to work its way inside.

Upstairs, the only sound comes from a dripping tap. Water has stained the enamel of the bath in a long streak that reaches the plughole. Though I try my hardest, I can't tighten the tap any further.

Her bed is made. Everything has been left in good order. Passing the dressing table, there's a faint whiff of lavender water – though I could easily be imagining it. I blow dust off a case from the top of the wardrobe and fill it with things she might need. In her place, I'd appreciate a change of clothes – a few familiar objects. Everything is where I expect it to be, all neatly ironed and folded.

It's been a while since I walked down these stairs carrying a suitcase. I turn the central heating on and swivel the thermostat to low – just enough to stop her pipes from freezing. And then I'm done.

A gust slams the front door behind me. The falling flakes have grown fatter, are on the very cusp of turning to snow. Back inside my car, I blow on my hands and take a moment to ready myself for the last leg of the journey.

It's a relief when the engine catches first time. The Fiat's heating has never been impressive – it always takes an age to warm up.

The road is getting slippery and I concentrate solely on making sure I stay on it. I'm trying not to let my imagination run on ahead. They must have been salting because everything gets much clearer as I approach the motorway. My car's top speed is laughable but it's doing its best. Oddly, I want to get there and yet I don't.

This will be the first time I've visited Mum in hospital.

She came to see me in the maternity unit just after Kate had been born. Visiting time had already begun and the other mums and newborns were being greeted by hordes of family. Talking and laughing, they assembled around each bed with their gifts like so many nativity scenes – without the animals. Flashes were going off every few minutes whilst I lay alone in my bed.

Mum was the very last visitor to appear. She was clutching not one but two bouquets of shop-bought flowers – white lilies and red roses separately enclosed in layers of cellophane. Such an unlikely combination.

Her kiss left my cheek wet. She thrust the flowers at me and I thanked her. The pallor of the lilies made the roses look bruised while the deep red of the roses exaggerated the frailness of the lilies. Their sickly scent caught in my throat. Though I appreciated the gesture, I did my best to avoid looking at them.

'You're looking well,' she said, 'considering.' She sat down heavily and patted my hand. 'How was it, then?'

I didn't want to give a blow-by-blow account so I just said, 'Fairly quick at the end. I'd only been here a couple of hours.'

'You were lucky.' Her lips seemed ready to elaborate on the

other ways it might have turned out but she thought better of it and covered it with a smile. Looking round the noisy room and back she asked, 'Where's the babby?'

'They're doing a few tests, apparently. Nothing to worry about, or so they said.' I'd tried to sound calm but I was seething and painfully aware of my powerless state; I could only lie there imagining them manhandling her delicate newly emerged body.

'Don't go upsetting yourself, lass. I 'spect they'll bring her back shortly.' When she rubbed my shoulder, her hair got in my face. I noticed how much more grey there was amongst the black. She looked like she'd just finished painting a ceiling.

Leaning back in her chair, she folded her arms, took her time in that way she does whilst silently taking stock of you. 'It's nice and cozy in here, anyroad.' With that she shrugged off her thick coat and draped it over the back of the chair revealing a green jersey top I'd not seen before. Once she'd unwound her blue-patterned scarf, she laid it across her lap – stroked it like a cat. I wondered if she was tempted to take off her shoes, release those small, swollen feet, like she always used to after she got home from work.

'I'm dying to see her,' she said. 'My first granddaughter, eh.' My brother Kevin had already produced three strapping sons, but they were an ocean away.

'I wish *he* could see her.' My words wobbled under their weight.

Her palm felt rough against the back of my hand. 'Don't suppose it crossed Duncan's mind you'd be more than three weeks early.' She gave a snort of a laugh. 'What with it being your first, an' all. He phoned me earlier – told me himself he's trying to get the first flight home he can.' Her hand squeezed harder. 'Not his fault is it, Lottie love?' As always, she'd leapt to Duncan's defence.

'I was talking about Dad,' I said.

'Oh.' Her hand lost its grip on mine. I noticed the way she hesitated before she said, 'Aye, your dad would've been pleased as punch to have a little granddaughter.' She rearranged the scarf. 'Little girl, eh?'

I shut my eyes and we sat in silence until Mum said, 'I'm sure they'll have a vase we can borrow somewhere. Eh, did they tell you what she weighed?'

'Three and a bit kilograms.'

She laughed. 'What's that in old money?'

Though it had only been a couple of hours it was a struggle to remember. 'I think they said seven pounds – around that anyway.' Sitting up further, everything felt raw but still I made the effort.

She sucked in her breath and said, 'Not bad for a prem.' Having worked in a maternity ward for several years, she knew about things like that. Leaning in close, she whispered, 'Did you have to have any stitches?'

'A couple – though it felt like more.'

'Salty water on a cotton wool pad works wonders. I 'spect they can give you a rubber ring to sit on if it gets bad.'

'I'm not sitting on something like that,' I told her

'And I'm just saying – it can help if it's a problem. Eh, you want to watch them toilet seats an' all – hospitals don't get cleaned properly these days. Course, in my day–'

'I'm being discharged tomorrow morning.'

'So soon?' Her mouth seemed to fold in on itself as she fought to suppress her opinion. Her hands smoothing the scarf in her lap with increasing speed, she took a noticeable breath before saying, 'Offer's still there if you'd like me to come and stay for a bit to help out. Believe me, you'll get dog-tired with all the feeding and changing. Poor Duncan will only just have got back from America – bound to still be jetlagged.'

'His flight was only six and a half hours the last time,' I told her. 'Besides, we've made all the arrangements. The au pair starts next week. She's a nice girl. French. She's had lots of experience with newborns. Besides, I've got maternity leave. You never know, I might even get round to finishing that novel.'

I saw the cynicism in her eyes. 'Wouldn't bank on it.' It was a remark you could take several ways and I'd learnt not to exclude any possibilities.

'Here we are then.' The chubby young nurse reappeared carrying Kate. 'All's fine with baby. She's fast asleep – good as gold.' They'd swaddled her in a pink blanket with only her face visible.

I wanted to tell the nurse to piss off but instead I said, 'Give her to me.' It was a struggle to add, 'Please.'

Mum looked at the nurse and together they conspired a smile. 'You want to make the most of her sleeping,' Mum said. 'She'll be awake soon enough.'

'I don't bloody care if she howls the fucking place down – just give her to me.' Amongst the visitors several heads had turned at that.

It did the trick – the nurse finally handed her over. They'd bound her up so tight it wasn't easy to unwrap her. I checked her head, her arms, legs, hands and finally her feet. There was a sticking plaster attached to one of her heels. 'What's that?' I demanded of the nurse.

'Oh, that's nothing,' she said, 'just her vitamin K jab.'

I was furious. 'How can she need an injection already?' Under my stare more colour crept into her young face, highlighting her ongoing battle with acne.

Mum intervened. 'It's routine, love. Stops them bleeding if they haven't got enough of it.' She shook my arm. 'Let's have a look at her then.'

I wanted to leap at them both. 'You should have asked me first.'

'Eh, but she's lovely,' Mum said. 'Will you look at those tiny little fingers. I never could get over how they can have long nails when they're only a few hours old.'

'But they're not, are they?' I said. 'In China they say they're one year old when they're born.'

Mum stopped cooing. 'Daft bloody idea, if you ask me.'

'Nine months would make a bit more sense,' the nurse added.

I allowed the pink blanket to drop to the floor. 'At least they acknowledge their prior existence,' I said. 'They don't immediately try to fit them into a bloody mould.'

Mum leant forward to mutter, 'Don't go upsetting yourself, Lottie. Nobody's going to take her away from you.'

Her calloused hand reached over to stroke Katie's fine head of hair. 'She looks just like you did when you were born. Those exact same blue eyes.'

'They could change,' I told her. 'They might end up any colour.'

I was right about that; within a few months little Katie's eyes turned grey-green exactly like Duncan's

With five or so miles still to go, something – a nagging intuition – creeps across my scalp, telling me I need to go faster or it could be too late. The Fiat doesn't tend to respond well to being pushed but I accelerate into the middle lane, holding fast to the wheel while the car braces itself for yet more buffeting by the heavy lorries and the tidal wave of spray in their wake.

A couple of miles further on, the traffic in front of me suddenly stops and I'm forced to brake hard. Snow has settled on the road and it's not easy to control the skid. All three lanes form a slow procession. There's no way to go any faster.

I move into the slow lane to turn off for the city. The snow is beginning to cover every horizontal surface. Caught unaware, the road ahead is reduced to two tyre tracks. The sign to the hospital is partly obscured; I only spot it at the last minute.

Parking isn't a problem; the car park has emptied out leaving snowy outlines where the cars had been. As I pull on the handbrake, I take a deep breath. I'm not ready for this by a long way. And I'm not even appropriately dressed.

Stepping out into slush, I regret my choice of footwear most of all. At my back, the wind rushes me on. They've spread salt nearer the main building and I have to sidestep the melt puddles. Beside the front entrance doors, a bin is overflowing with dog-ends. The snow is doing its best to hide the evidence.

When I step inside, a current of hot air takes my breath

away. With purpose, I stride along the corridors, the overhead signage guiding me this way and that.

My heels ring out against the hard floor. I pass a long frieze depicting stick-men doctors and stick-women standing next to tipped-up beds with scribble-faced patients. Who doesn't love children's drawings? They do their best to soften the edges of this place.

I take the lift and then make a right turn. Following my enquiry, a young nurse points me to a recess off the corridor. 'Take a seat,' she says. 'Someone will be along shortly.'

At first, I perch on the edge of my chair. Time passes but no one comes and so I sit further back. In desperation, I begin to flick through some old magazines – taking nothing in but the airbrushed, smiling faces.

A short woman wearing scrubs calls my name and tells me to follow her. We navigate along various corridors until we get to a bed in an alcove with its curtains pulled around. She yanks them apart like a showbiz assistant: Ta-daa!

Mum is lying on a metal-framed bed. It's hard to recognise her; she looks older and so insubstantial – hardly able to dent the mattress. 'I'll leave you to it,' the nurse tells me.

'I'm here,' I say. When I take hold of her hand, it feels chilly and lifeless, then it gives itself away with a slight flutter. Her eyelids flicker before they half open. Her mouth struggles to form a word. 'Kevin?'

'No, Mum – it's Charlotte.' I add, 'Your daughter,' in case there's any confusion.

'Lottie?'

'That's right.' She closes her eyes. I reach up to the thin

skin at her temples and with the backs of my fingers stroke down towards the crosshatched folds beneath her chin. There's movement beneath her sparse eyelashes. Is she awake or dreaming? I want to tell her so many things but I don't know how to begin.

Before I open my mouth, a striking Asian woman steps inside our curtain tent and introduces herself as Dr Azziz – Mum's surgeon. She apologises for the fact that they've had to bump Mum's operation a couple of times. 'On busy days like this we have to prioritise,' she tells me. It seems they've been starving Mum for hours in anticipation. 'I'm pleased to say we've now managed to find her a slot.' She smiles. 'It's a fairly straightforward operation; we don't anticipate too many problems.'

'But that means there could be some?'

This time, her smile is more strained. 'Sadly, there are no guarantees. The odds are very much in your mother's favour.' She steps back – eager to be off. 'We'll speak again afterwards.' She touches my shoulder. 'The porters will be along shortly.'

I'm allowed to follow behind as they wheel her along the corridor into another room. A medic in a different shade of scrubs comes in; this one is very tall and white. He clears his throat and says, 'I'm Mr Foreman, the anaesthetist. You must be the patient's daughter.'

'Yes. It took me ages to get up here,' I add for no good reason. They've let me stay with her – a worry in itself. 'The weather out there is a nightmare.'

'So I hear.' He pulls a sympathetic face then looks away

towards the window with its falling snow. 'If you wouldn't mind stepping back a little.'

I watch the man's gloved hand hold a syringe high to the light, measuring the line of clear liquid against gradations too far away for me to see. A brief, professional squirt checks its flow. 'This is simply to relax her,' he tells me. Looking at Mum, it's hard to see how she could be any more relaxed.

'Sorry to intrude.' A pale-skinned woman is awkwardly suspended between being in the room and not. 'Mr Isherwood would like a quick word…'

He sighs. The instrument clatters back to its previous position on a metal tray. The anaesthetist holds up a gloved finger. 'Excuse me for just a moment, Mrs, ah – ' Her name disappears with him.

Mum's been left under the callous spotlight in the half-cocked bed – given a reprieve, a small stay of execution.

I wait – the two of us wait. Lost for words, time bunches up around us.

The anaesthetist comes back. 'Sorry about that …' is delivered into my face, not hers. 'Where was I?' Deciding to abandon the effort required to explain, he strides over to the trolley, tears off his gloves, jettisons them into a bag-bin then snaps on another pair.

So this is it. I have to turn away. Outside the window a charcoal sky droops under too much weight. When I look back, he's ripping open a small pack to extract a wipe that smells of surgical spirit. He rubs it back and forth over the same puckering spot on her arm.

The syringe is once more held to the light. 'Okay,' he says, 'you're just going to feel a little prick,' a comedy line that, despite the circumstances, makes me smile. I nearly miss the one swift movement it takes to puncture her skin. Mum doesn't respond as his determined thumb applies the pressure necessary to send that clear liquid into her bloodstream.

Satisfied, he steps back and makes space for me.

'It's going to be fine.' I squeeze her hand – not too hard. 'You'll feel much better soon. I promise.'

In a matter of minutes she's wheeled out through propped doors; I get a glimpse of two masked men waiting to receive her. Ahead of me, Mum is guided past a sign that reads: NO UNAUTHORISED PERSONS BEYOND THE RED LINE, and then she's gone.

And I'm back to where I was before – waiting. Above my head, the fly that's been buzzing around suddenly ricochets off the florescent tube; with a blunted crack it drops onto the stack of magazines. Lying on its back, it looks dead; though its tiny legs are still twitching – reflexes not knowing when to give up.

Someone in scrubs pushes through the heavy doors; around her neck a mask is slung like a bow tie. 'Miss Preece?' she asks getting closer. I'm the only one in here so it's an easy guess. With her hair covered, I almost don't recognise her as Dr Azziz – the elegant surgeon I spoke to earlier.

I stand up and duck my head back down until the room lightens again. She fixes me in her dark and knowing eyes and I wait upon her verdict. 'I'm afraid it's going to be a little while longer. You might want to grab a coffee or something.'

'But I thought – you said she'd be out by now.' For some reason I look at my watch, as I might if an Uber is late arriving.

'We've had a few complications.' Her sterile hand touches my shoulder, pats it almost. 'Not unexpected at your mother's age. It's all under control now.' Those sculptured eyebrows drop down to make way for a serious smile. 'All things considered, she's doing fine. We'll let you know once the operation is over. With luck you should be able to see her before too long.'

The mention of luck does little to reassure me. Dr Azziz turns away abruptly and continues along the corridor, her plastic shoes a rhythm of squelches against the polished floor. Watching her go, I get that feeling I used to get when the pilot would circulate amongst the passengers: very good of you to be sociable and all that, but who's been left to fly the damned plane?

I make myself breathe deeply, right from the abdomen. Three times: long draw in, with a steady out. My brain begins to feel too light. They're sealed in nowadays – the pilots that is – no more cute kids with their dimpled hands inching towards the vital controls. They work in teams when they're operating. I expect she just needs a pee or something – doctors are human, after all.

I've been relieved of duty in a way; given time to get something to eat or drink, stretch my legs even.

The Kindness of Strangers

Outside, right outside in the freezing air, the snow is falling like it means business. Near the main entrance a huddle of dressing-gowned smokers perch in one of the see-through bus shelters. I hear them laugh. One man is facing the others; he's leaning on the stand suspending his drip with a casual air, like a comic with an elbow on his microphone. Together they release lungfuls of smoke into the growing darkness.

When I turn on my phone it tells me I've missed several calls, one of them from Duncan of all people.

There's also a WhatsApp message from Kate.

Went ok but I ran out of time near the end. In the pub drinking – only ½ bitter. B says hi. Speak soon. xxx for Gran

The smiley face she added looks up at me like an accusation. I remind myself there is no point in worrying her at this stage; she still has two more exams to sit.

When I return Duncan's call, his wife answers his mobile. 'Hi, Charlotte,' she says, her voice is saccharine over espresso.

'Dunc's out back playing with the boys – they're real excited about the snow, as you can imagine.' She's probably wearing a cashmere sweater that sets off her fresh-faced good looks – some pastel shade that complements her blonde hair. *Dunc* is bad – why can't she use his proper name? 'I'll go give him a shout,' she says.

'No. They're obviously having fun – please don't disturb them on my account. Honestly, he can ring me back another –'

'I'm happy to go get him for you; it's no problem. Besides it's nearly dark out there and the boys still have homework to do.' Her laugh is brittle. 'Though they're hoping for no school tomorrow. If you hold on, I'll just –'

'Don't!' I say too forcibly. 'It's fine, honestly. I'll call him tomorrow.'

I hang up to make my point.

Thick flakes are swimming around the high security lights, others cling to my hair or melt into my eyes and mouth. It's freezing and I need to get my circulation going. Keeping to where they've spread salt, I weave an aimless path around the handful of frosted-up cars that are left. The usual stunted shrubs have been glamorised by a generous dusting of snow.

It's not long before I'm back to square one. I draw level with the smokers in the shelter. Breathing in the tobacco-stained air, I envy them this solidarity, that *we-don't-give-a-crap* attitude. I gave up smoking as soon as I fell pregnant with Kate and haven't had the nerve or sheer stupidity to start again.

A muddle? A foggle? No, a ca-cough-ony of smokers.

All heads turn towards a shrieking siren. An ambulance

careers onto the perimeter road; its blue lights strobe our retinas as it hurtles along and then pulls up outside the Casualty entrance. Doors are flung open. Someone's life is in the balance on the stretcher they're hastily wheeling inside. Within a few short minutes the doors are slammed shut and they're off on another rescue mission – everyday heroes, for sure.

Witnessing such urgency has unnerved me. While I've been wasting time out here, everything could be going wrong up there.

The possibility pushes me right back through the glass doors. I power down the corridors towards the steel faces of the lifts.

The disembodied voice announces my floor as I step out. Wringing my hands with more anti-bacterial goo, I make my way to the now familiar waiting area and its line of hard chairs.

This time someone else is there and he's taken my seat – the one nearest the corridor. I know it's unreasonable to be annoyed – how could he have known? I sit down two chairs away from him and stare out of the wide window at the last glowerings of the day.

My watch tells me I was absent for twenty-two minutes. Anything could have happened.

Turning my head, I notice the intruder is sprawled right out. He looks quite young, though half his face is buried in a hoody. He's sitting low, almost falling out of the chair; his long legs are crossed at the ankle and end in dirty trainers. His hands are pushed deep into both pockets. He hasn't looked up, hasn't acknowledged my presence.

Five minutes elapse and no one's come to find me. I'm

learning about this waiting routine – how it saps your energy and leaves you both anxious and bored. There should be a word for it. Banxious Anxbored? I don't suppose they came to get me; I probably wasn't missed.

To pass the time, I stare out at the city and the falling snow until everything blurs into nothing. My eyes are drawn towards the wall opposite; I try to stop them wandering towards the only object that relieves its blankness – a small Constable print in a mock-wood frame depicting the minor calamity of a cart stuck in a shallow river. The painter, the cart driver and possibly those overblown trees may no longer exist but, thanks to Constable's faithful rendering, their facsimiles will continue in perpetuity.

The young man sighs – it's a long one that signals the need to communicate; one of those I'm-going-to-say-something-banal-to-pass-the-time type of sighs. I pick up a magazine and pretend to read it. Then I remember the fly; it must have dropped off onto the floor. My glance sweeps the floor and there it is – a black spec of nothing. Dead.

Movement catches my attention. The boy has taken off his jacket and is hanging it across the back of the chair. I pretend interest in what Katie said to Damian. It's really over this time or so the strap-line says. Roy Orbison takes his cue and starts to whine out *It's over* in my head. On idle my brain tends to throw up music like it's salmonella. It's seldom a great tune like Roy's; more often it's the crap they play at the end of wedding receptions – the stuff that keeps on swirling away in the void like astronauts' shit. The real menace of those silly tunes is the power they have to reduce any occasion to a farce.

The boy clears his throat not once, but twice. I will him to stay silent but he doesn't. 'These places, eh.' His accent is local.

Damn! I want to ignore him but can't. 'Yeah.' I elongate the word so it sits there like a log blocking the way. I'm careful to make absolutely no eye contact.

'So bloody stuffy in here,' he says.

'Must cost a fortune to heat.' My mouth is exercising free will.

His long legs are bent, both knees are doing that pent-up shuddering thing only young, bored men seem to do. 'No bugger tells you anythin'.'

'I suppose they're busy,' I say. 'Getting on with their jobs – saving people's lives and all that.'

He shrugs. 'Yeah – I guess.' Abruptly, his denim-clad legs stand up and cross the room in front of me. He walks over to the sealed, probably triple-glazed, window. 'Pitch black out there now,' he says. He's tall, really tall. The top of his head is thick with spiky, dark hair while the sides are almost shaved.

'Yes,' costs me more than it should.

Checking his phone he says, 'Rush hour, I suppose.'

Beyond him, I can see wavering strings of red and white lights. 'When did it stop being rush hour and become crawl hour?'

He gives a little snort at that, leans farther into the window. 'Good question.'

Another siren whines, its urgent pitch penetrates every invisible layer. I can see his reflection. He has a nice face, handsome even. Is he staring out at the world, or at himself in it? He rests both elbows on the ledge, one hand supporting his jaw. 'It looks so different from up here.'

'From in here, too.'

'Yeah.' The upturned sole of his shoe is moving to its own beat. 'Makes you think about things and, like. Everything.' I nod in agreement though he won't have seen. 'I guess that's what you do,' he mumbles into the glass. 'When things, like, happen.' I start to wonder what brought him here and why he's staying. The world of my crisis has been breached; I'm not the only one going through this tonight.

He's probably a couple of years or so younger than Kate – about the same age her brother would have been if he'd lived. The poor boy looks lost; I have to fight the instinct to put an arm around him.

He gives a heavy sigh and then the two of us fall silent.

It's impossible to prevent my thoughts from running on to how things might have been so different if our son had survived.

Guilty as Charged

The boy's loud grunt interrupts my thoughts. Eyes shut, he rearranges his limbs and settles down to snooze quietly again. I hear his regular breathing. How can he sleep, sprawled out on a hard chair, head lolling to one side? Never mind that he's waiting for news about someone he must really care about. I envy him being able to switch off like that.

To relieve the monotony and the pressure on my backside, I stand up. It's a short walk along the corridor to the bank of gaudy vending machines that must be there for the convenience of the staff. I choose a Kit-Kat and a white tea. When I press the button something grey and unappealing dribbles into the cup.

The first sip burns the roof of my mouth and tastes even worse than I expected. I sit down and warm my hands on the cup's corrugated sides and wait for it to cool down a little.

A thought keeps niggling at me – should I phone Kate? It's hard to think what I might say; right now everything is still up in the air. Better then to wait until the news is more definitive.

To keep myself hydrated, I swallow a few mouthfuls of tea

and discover it's gone from scalding to tepid. I want to throw the rest away but there's nowhere to do that without making a mess. Checking my watch, I decide it's time I went back to where they can find me if there's any news.

I can't throw the rest of the tea in the wire bin so I dump it onto a dried-out plant that's sitting on the windowsill; it looks like it could do with a drink.

The tea runs straight through the pot, out of the bottom and down the wall onto the floor. And I have nothing to wipe up the mess. It occurs to me this poor plant might be some sort of desert dweller on a strict watering limit and I might have just administered a fatal overdose.

I can't undo what's done. The grey puddle on the floor grows accusing fingers that point to me as the culprit. I turn my back and slink away.

I'm reminded of an incident during a teenage party at my friend's house; we discovered too late that a drunken boy had chucked vodka into her parents' fancy fish tank so that they could join in the fun. By the time I left, several fish were already floating belly up on the surface.

A nurse with skinny legs is walking towards me on thick-soled shoes. 'Miss Preece?'

'Yes.' I try this again in a lower register. 'Yes, that's me.'

'They're going to transfer your mother to the Recovery Ward as soon as they can.' She says this in a flat sort of tone like a supermarket announcement.

I stand up. 'So the operation is over?'

'I imagine so.' Her freckled face is blank.

She imagines so? 'Is she alright? Did everything go okay?'

'Sorry – they only asked me to let you know she's going to be transferred as soon as they can find a bed for her. Recovery Ward's currently full, so there's going to be a short holdup while they sort everybody out.'

She starts to retreat – eager to get on with something else. 'I'm sure someone will come and have a word with you shortly.' Before I can ask any more questions she holds up a hand. 'We're rushed off our feet tonight. This sort of weather always brings them in thick and fast.'

'Do you know if my mum's regained consciousness?'

'I'm really sorry – I don't. I've only just come on duty.' She turns away and this time makes good her escape through the swinging door.

When I kick at the wall, the lad says, 'I'm sure she'll be okay.'

How the hell can he say that? I'm angry when I look at him full in the face for the first time and register how young he is. I say, 'Maybe they've done all they can for her.'

His shoulders perform a slight shrug and he looks down at the floor; his unruly hair flops leaving only the tip of his nose exposed. He was trying to help. I ought to reciprocate – ask him to tell me his story, offer a little understanding or companionship, but I don't. I've no energy left for anyone else's personal crisis.

Venturing outside an hour or so later the night sky has cleared and is speckled with stars. There's almost a full moon and, due to all the lying snow, everything glows with an eerie light.

'Your mother is fast asleep,' the nurse-in-charge had said. And, 'Try not to worry; we'll be keeping a very close eye on her. Someone will call you if there's any change.' Did she use those exact words? It might have been: 'We'll call *when* there's any change.'

Do the two mean the same thing?

'Why don't you go and get some rest.' She'd placed a hand on my shoulder – a motherly gesture despite the similarity in our ages. 'You look like you need a good night's sleep,' was more than a suggestion. It crossed my mind she might give me a push if I resisted.

I try to open the car door, but it won't budge. Damn it! I yank harder and this time there's a tearing sound as I wrench it free. A fine line of snow falls down my collar and the cold reality of it sends a shock right through me.

I'm not sure I'm thinking clearly anymore. Except for a Kit-Kat, I haven't eaten for hours. My head feels crowded and close and there's a growing pain over my eyes that could herald a migraine though I never get them. What if they lose my number? They could misdial. Given how busy they are, they might forget to ring me.

The car starts first time; I want to give it a pat for its good behaviour. My eyes are heavy but I need to concentrate to get to the hotel I booked from faraway, snow-free London.

I'll have to go through all the crap of registering before I'm given a key card. I wish I could lie down right this minute and just close my eyes on this whole sorry day.

A New Dawn

I wake with a start around 4.40, or so the clock on the radio informs me. Reassured, I doze off for a bit longer and when I check again the numbers read 6:55. Time I was up.

Turning on the television for the weather report, it's a shock to recognise Michael dressed in a flak jacket and wearing a tin helmet. He's crouching behind the wall of some ruined building. The white letters across his chest declaring he's PRESS – they stand out like the easiest of targets. His face is streaked with dust. Just above a whisper he speaks to camera – describes in horrifying details what is happening around him. He tells the viewers he's embedded with the opposition militia. He must be delighted that his frontline reports are now reaching a wider audience.

I wince when a stray bullet sings past his head and hits the wall behind. The men around him return fire and the noise drowns out what he's saying. I've always been fearful for his safety; it's not something you can switch off just like that. They've stopped shooting. Someone is shouting orders in a language I don't understand until he translates. It seems they're planning to advance to the next street. 'Here we go,' Michael says as they make their move. He's breathless with fear and excitement.

My own heart is racing. With the time difference, this footage can't be live. I'm sure he must have survived or they wouldn't be showing it; at least I don't think they would. In any case I can't watch any more. Right now it's impossible to handle another life and death situation.

It's a relief to change channels. Getting over our break-up was far harder than I'd imagined. I certainly didn't expect him to pop up on the morning news with no warning. It's no wonder he found it hard to adjust; to behave like a regular human being when he was at home with us. Life in an ordinary household in Camden was always going to be far too tame after where he'd just been, what he'd just seen. I got that, did my best to understand but in the end we'd had to concede that our lives were too far apart to bridge the gap.

The local news is full of minor weather-related disasters – the kind I can handle. It ends with a weather update – it seems the main roads are mostly clear but there are dozens of jack-knifed trucks and abandoned cars on approach roads. I'm advised not to make any unnecessary journeys.

With the lights on, my hotel room has everything I want, and not much I really need. My throat's sore. In the fake wood minibar I find two small and expensive bottles of water – fizzy not still.

I can hear the gurgle of the internal waste – the building's not mine. More splooshing and flushing marks the start of the day like an alternative dawn chorus.

When I'm decent, I open the curtains and am shocked by the depth of the snow that's glittering under the lights. A set of human footprints have left a trail under my window. At a guess, I'd say they go down about six centimetres. It looks much deeper where it's drifted against walls.

Will I be able to get to the hospital? I guess there's only one way to find out.

Once again the Fiat starts first time. 'Well done,' I tell it out loud. We crunch down the driveway onto the B road. Further on, I'm relieved to discover the main roads have been ploughed and gritted. I pass a string of abandoned vehicles on the side of the road but thankfully nothing blocks my route.

The hospital is much busier this morning. Several people are being wheeled around with casts on various limbs.

On the advice of the receptionist, I go back to the same waiting area. This time it's hard to find a seat. Looking around, I half expect to see the boy from last night and am disappointed when I don't. I hope the news was good for him. After a half hour wait, they tell me I can see Mum.

Her bed is still curtained off. I step inside. Under stiff white sheets, she's propped up by pillows and dressed in the blue and white nightie I brought in. Her eyes are closed. Someone's arranged her arms alongside her. It looks like she's already been laid out.

When I check, I'm relieved that her chest is moving up and down. I'm surprised to see a series of quick movements beneath her eyelids – she must be dreaming.

'Mum?'

She doesn't answer.

My mobile rings. Shit – I'd forgotten to turn it off. I search for it amongst the layers of junk in my bag, while I picture all the X-ray or radiotherapy machines malfunctioning and beginning to melt through the ward floors. Maybe a fiery magma chamber has started to open up beneath the hospital, like a Bond-villain's island; its fierce red flow already filling up the basement.

'Phone,' she croaks, eyes still shut tight.

'It's okay, Mum,' I tell her. 'Nothing to worry about.'

'Harry's here.' The tip of her tongue emerges. I watch it glide across her top lip. 'Late again – his dinner will be dried up.'

'Sssh, don't worry about that now.'

Her mouth moves like she's rehearsing words and then she whispers, 'Not now.'

I place my hand on her forehead. It feels chilly despite the overpowering heat. Is that good or bad? 'You need to rest, Mum. Everything's okay – the operation's over.' I kiss her brow. 'We can talk later.'

Her eyes flutter then her breathing gets harsher. Though her mouth is closed, she gives the deepest of sighs, like the effort of staying awake is too much.

Her chest sinks and I hold my breath until I see it rise and fall again. I fight the urge to wake her. Her next sigh is loud and from the heart. I watch the muscles in her face go slack, see her cares retreat as she settles back into what could be unconsciousness.

Should I ring the buzzer? The machines around the bed are humming – they must be sending information to someone. No alarm has been triggered so I think she must be just resting. And why not – after all, she's been through such a lot.

Watching her, I'm reminded of a saying of my dad's, which he alone seemed to find highly amusing. 'Roll on death,' he'd say. 'Let's have a long lie in.'

One particular Sunday morning sticks in my mind. I reckon I must have been about eight or nine at the time. Dad had just come downstairs in his pyjamas. Looking up from the jigsaw I'd been fiddling with on the kitchen table, I giggled at the way his normally slicked-back hair was sticking up at the front.

After picking up the Sunday Mirror from the mat, he poured himself a cup of tea and, wedging the rolled-up newspaper under one arm, he concentrated on the cup as he climbed the stairs.

Hands on hips, Mum stopped what she was doing to demand, 'When do *I* get a bloody lie-in?'

He paused halfway up the stairs, to shout back, 'Well, what's stopping you?'

'Only the ironing, the vegetables for dinner not done, the kitchen floor not swept and all the rest ont.' She said it in that voice – the one that if it were a smell would be nail-varnish remover.

He didn't reply. The bedroom door banged shut. I looked at her red face and the yellow gloves that gave her cartoon hands. She turned her back and carried on with the washing up.

Instead of offering to help, I concentrated on the missing pieces of the roof. I'd already finished the walls of the cottage and the long spiky flowers in the front garden. It wasn't easy. I did my best to ignore the clatter of the ironing board being put up. In my side vision I saw her begin to iron with a vengeance.

I'd just located the final piece of chimney when Dad came downstairs again; this time he was fully dressed. 'Right then,' he said rubbing his hands together. 'How about I go and pick some of that purple sprouting you like? Reckon it's more or less ready. I'll do a pot of tatters after that; let you put your feet up for a bit.'

Mum said nothing.

'Come on, love. I've said, I'll go and pick–'

'I heard what you said.' Mum stared down at the ironing board, not at him.

'Carol there's no need.' He said this in a gentler tone. 'I've offered to give you a hand. What more do you want?'

She stopped what she was doing and the smell of scorched cloth began to fill the room. I'd never seen her cry before. Wiping her dripping nose with the back of her hand, she said, 'More than this.'

When she turned to look at us, I wished she hadn't; I didn't want to witness how her red and angry eyes went from him to me like she was seeing us both properly for the first time. Judging us.

Dad grabbed the iron before his best shirt could burst into flames. The scorch mark it had left would never come out. Mum shook her head. In a sad voice she said it again, 'More than just this.'

My mouth turned down by itself and I started to cry. I hated the whining noise I was making but I couldn't help it. Dad came over to me. 'There, there, lass. No need to fret so much, Lottie love.' He put his heavy arm around my shoulder. 'Your mam's just a bit upset, that's all.'

'Oh – that's all, is it?' Mum was so angry she could barely get the words out. She was trembling all over. I knew Dad should be cuddling her and not me. 'I'm sorry, Mummy,' I said.

'Aye, we're all sorry, aren't we?' she snapped. Then she walked across the room and slammed the back door behind her. I felt the rush of air on my wet face.

'Don't go worrying,' Dad said. ''Spect it's her time of life – if you get my meaning? She'll get over it shortly.' He gave my shoulder a squeeze and pretended to be calmer than I knew he was. 'You get on with your puzzle, I'll go and talk to her.'

I heard them rowing in the garden. I did my best to concentrate on the sky, matching the light bits up and then the darker blue section – there was only that left. I tried turning the next piece every way I could but it wouldn't fit. In the end I jammed it in where it didn't want to go. I didn't care anymore; I just wanted to finish the thing, even though I knew it was wrong.

Where her lips meet, a line of tiny bubbles vibrate with the air passing in and out. On the inside of her arm a cross of blue tape holds the cannula that holds the tubes delivering the clear liquids that make up the necessary ingredients of life. It doesn't boil down to much; she could be a plant in a greenhouse for all this equipment cares.

I see a shadowy hand looming behind the curtains. They part and Duncan of all people steps inside as though my unconscious has just summoned him.

I'm dumbfounded. A few flakes of snow still cling to this hair. 'Hi,' he says. Then nodding towards the bed. 'How is she?'

I find my voice. 'I don't know. No one knows. I gather it's in the lap of the gods, or the next throw of the dice – choose your fucking cliché.'

'Right,' he says.

We both stare down at Mum. For the zillionth time I check the tube snaking down to her arm; it's hard to tell whether the clear liquid inside it is still moving.

'So, did they give you the – you know.' He clears his throat. 'The prognosis?'

'Not yet.' He's forcing me to think more than I want to.

He shakes his head. 'Jesus, she looks terrible.'

'You could try saying something to keep my spirits up.'

'Sorry. It's just Kate seemed to think... And now, looking at her, it's much worse, far worse than I expected.'

'For Christ's sake Duncan, this is hardly making me feel better.'

'What do you want me to say?'

'How about something a bit more positive.'

There's a beat before he says, 'I see she's lost the weight she was always meaning to.'

Someone else is trying to part the curtains. When it's drawn aside, a different doctor is standing there. He's youngish, tall with an ultra-serious expression. 'Miss Preece?'

My stomach almost liquefies. 'Yes.'

'Good afternoon. I understand you are Mrs Preece's next-of-kin?' A phrase divorced from reality.

'Yes, I suppose I am.' It's hard to keep my voice steady. 'I'm her daughter.'

'I'm Mister Gaidhani. I'm the Senior Registrar.' His accent

is Indian. I expect him to shake my hand but he doesn't. He studies the notes in his hand and then glances at Mum. Repeats this action several times. The middle finger of his free hand rubs at his forehead like he's trying to make up his mind.

Then it stops. I think he's about to say something crucial, but instead he looks at Duncan and says. 'And you, sir are also family?'

'Um.' Nonplused, Duncan tells him. 'I'm her son-in-law – or, I should say, her ex-son-in-law.' Raising an eyebrow, he nods towards the exit with all the subtlety of a bouncer. 'Would you like me to, you know…'

I grab the arm of his coat. 'I want you to stay.'

'Well now, Miss Preece,' the registrar's fingers tap the edge of the chart. 'I expect you've been told there was a bit of drama during your mother's surgery. The good news is they managed to stop the bleeding and, as you see, your mother's condition would appear to be reasonably stable at the moment.'

I wait for the bad news.

'This was a serious operation – serious whatever the age of the patient. It's too early to make any predictions.' He looks at me like he's looking over spectacles, though he's not wearing any. 'I'm afraid we have to bear in mind your mother's age and physical frailty. Nothing is certain at this stage. It all depends on her resilience. It may be hard to accept but we simply have to wait and see.'

'How long before she's likely to wake up?' Duncan asks before I get a chance.

'Well now – what with the effects of the anesthetic and the drugs we are giving her to manage the pain, I think it likely she will be fairly unresponsive for quite some time. Several more hours I'd expect – possibly longer.'

'Can I stay here?' I ask. 'I mean, I don't need to stick to the official visiting hours?'

'Under these circumstances, we like to be reasonably flexible.' Alarm bells start ringing in my head.

'If we go and get something to eat,' Duncan says, 'could someone call Charlotte if she wakes up?'

'Certainly.' The doctor turns his all-too-knowing eyes on me. 'If you'd like to leave us your mobile number, Miss Preece, we'll notify you if there's any change in her condition.'

Food for Thought

We're in a restaurant, at a table for two. Every window showcases the snow falling against the dark flanks of the buildings opposite. The room is warm, and hums with quiet conversations; white-aproned waiters cross back and forth with loaded trays in a practiced dance.

I check my phone. No messages or missed calls from the hospital or any unknown numbers. There are plenty of bars so the signal's okay.

'Who's having de cod?' I raise a finger. 'Here we are, signora.' In front of me the waiter places a white plate containing a crisp-skinned fish on a bed of pureed peas. To one side, wedges of chips have been built up like Jenga blocks. The combined aroma of oregano and garlic rises to greet me. 'Careful, de plate is very hot.' Is he genuinely Italian? I listen for an unguarded syllable that might give him away.

'De duck breast for you, signore.' On Duncan's plate artfully scattered wild mushrooms surround the plumpness of the duck and its bloody juices. Glass softly clinks against glass as he tops up our mineral water. 'Buono appetito. Enjoy.'

I'm hungry and the first mouthful tastes divine. When I look up, Duncan's busy eating. I watch the way he chews and notice again the lines fanning out from his eyes. Though there's a new heaviness to his eyelids, he's aging damned near perfectly. I stop eating and lay down my cutlery. 'This doesn't seem right.'

'What's not right?' His grey eyes show a hint of annoyance. 'Eating proper hot food? Drinking from a glass and not a paper cup?'

'Everything. All of it. You and me. This whole thing.'

'For Christ's sake, Lottie, give yourself a break.' I'm not sure I believe his exasperation. 'We're only five minutes away. They've promised they'll ring if things change. You're exhausted. You need to look after yourself too, you know.'

This hits a nerve: 'I can do that just fine, thank you very much.'

He holds up both hands. 'Only trying to help.'

'I know you are, and I'm grateful, but–'

'But what? *But* you're not hungry? *But* you prefer to eat shit hospital canteen food? *But* you just want me to piss off and leave you alone?'

'No need to get angry. I can't help it – I feel guilty; and not just about this.'

His warm fingers pin down my hand. He shakes it. 'I'm very fond of the old girl too you know, always have been. I always do my best to pop in for a chat and a cup of tea when I'm up this way.'

'I know – she's told me.'

'It's not your fault she's ill. She's almost eighty. These things are bound to happen.'

'She's only seventy-eight.' It seems important to make the distinction.

'I keep thinking, you know, that I should have tried harder. Should have been kinder.'

After a while he passes me his napkin.

I hand it back and find a tissue in my bag instead. I can't decide whether to tell him anything, or everything. No. It's not the right time.

I check my phone. Nothing. I take a sip of water and my empty stomach gurgles back at me. The smell of my food is too seductive. I pick up my discarded cutlery and cut a sliver of cod away. 'You know, this tastes great,' I tell him. 'I've had nothing but soggy crap to eat for two days and I'm starving.'

'I got up at five-thirty,' he says between mouthfuls. 'Drive up was a nightmare. The M1 was closed just north of Nottingham.' His knife releases more blood. 'Took me ages to find a way round.'

'I'm not sure I thanked you,' I say. 'I may not have shown it, but I am truly grateful that you came here today. And I most definitely don't want you to piss off.'

'Good to hear.' His smile could always disarm me. 'That's settled then,' he declares. 'Let's just enjoy our meal.'

While I eat, my thoughts run back to when I was about four or five. Mum and I went Christmas shopping together – just the two of us. She'd promised we might go and have a bite to eat in a café afterwards if it wasn't too crowded. I was excited because it felt like a special occasion. Mum had pinned back her hair and was wearing lipstick and her brand new beige coat. The floral scarf round her throat smelt of lavender – what she always referred to as eau-de-cologne. On the top deck, sitting side-by-side, we looked out through the filthy window at the swaying coloured lights and the people milling on the pavements. I don't recall getting off the bus but I do remember how she held my hand too tightly and a man telling her, 'Sorry, pet – we've completely run out. You could try Woolies.'

Inside the big shop, I was disappointed when we walked straight past the sweet counter. My stretched-too-far arm was hurting around the shoulder, so when she bent forward to look at something behind glass, I managed to slip my hand out of hers and rub away at it. People kept pushing and bumping into me but I dutifully followed when that beige coat moved off.

We walked out into the street. At the crossing, I offered up my hand again but the brown leather glove on the end of the sleeve failed to open. I looked up then at her turned-away face and saw that her hair was too long and too light.

The coat crossed over the road without me, her curls spilling over the wide collar and bouncing along until the crowd swallowed her – someone else's mummy.

I'd been following a stranger. Transfixed on the edge of the pavement next to the busy road, I had no idea what to do or which way to turn in the crowd. I kept scanning the coats that were coming and going, trying to find one that matched hers.

I don't remember much about the moment when she found me except that she was cross with me. What's stayed with me is my mistake – that sensation of looking up at the woman I had mistaken for Mum. How I had failed to recognise my own mother.

We order coffee and it comes with a plate of petit fours. I choose a tiny chocolate concoction and leave the rest for Duncan. 'These are so good,' he tells me. 'Are you sure I can't tempt you?'

On our way back, we pass a shop window full of televisions and stop to look at silent footage of cars stuck in drifts, jack-knifed lorries lying on their side with their loads disgorged into the snow. All manner of cans, beer barrels, even office supplies are strewn in the open.

'Yesterday, they had shots of happy children sledging,' Duncan says.

'From decorative to disaster inside twenty-four hours.' I look down at my inappropriate shoes. 'A bit of snow falls and it's treated like a national emergency.'

In a silly American voice he says, 'Raise our status to Defcon White.'

'Hang on, White means the threat's ridiculously bad – Armageddon is just around the corner.'

'No!' He frowns. 'White can't be that bad surely. It's too pale and boring – like a Jane Austin heroine.'

'I know you're just trying to provoke me.' I dig him in the ribs; he slips and I have to grab his arm. 'Sorry, that was harder than I intended.'

Duncan chuckles. 'Big bully.'

Muffled by my bag, it takes a minute to register my phone is ringing. The screen displays Kate's number. I decide not to mention the fact that her father's standing right next to me.

'It went much better than I thought,' she says without prompting.' I can hear people talking in the background. 'Fingers crossed I've done enough for a pass at least.'

'Well done!'

'So yeah, only one more to worry about now.'

Duncan goes to say something. 'Shush!' I put a finger to my lips and he literally backs off.

Kate tells me she's planning to come up on the train at the weekend – promises to text me her arrival time two long days away. I'm about to hint that things might be more serious than we thought when she says, 'I've sent Gran a get-well card. Found one of bluebells in a wood. She always says they're her favourite flowers.'

I picture this task on a to-do list that might include 'buy milk' and 'revise Avogadro's number' or 'Examples of Irreversible Process'.

'That's nice,' is all I say in reply.

'I thought of sending the card to the hospital, but I didn't know the ward number or anything, so I sent it to her house instead so it's there when she gets home. Should I get her some flowers? Maybe something to eat might be better. Not chocolates, I know. Fruit? What do you think she'd like to cheer her up?'

An innocent enough question. 'I shouldn't worry,' I tell her. 'Mum's got everything she needs at the moment.'

At her end there are raised voices, then a woman's shrieking laugh. 'Listen, I'd better go,' she says. 'Love you lots.'

'Me too,' I say to the disengaged tone.

'That was Kate.'

Duncan nods. 'Guessed as much.'

'I still haven't told her how serious things are with Mum. Thought I wouldn't just yet.'

'Probably for the best.' He says this without as much conviction as I would have liked.

We walk on, are nearly at the end of the road before either of us speaks. 'Getting back to that whole Defcon White thing, what were you going to tell me?'

'Okay, well.' Before he can take the piss, I say, 'Let me put it in context. I once researched the official American Defense Conditions because, in my last book – which I'll assume you haven't read – I have a character who likes reading thrillers to his girlfriend when they're in bed.'

'As one does.'

'Anyway, I found out they quite often get the sequence wrong in films.'

'Really?' He looks unconvinced. 'I mean that's got to be the easiest thing in the world to check.'

'You'd think so, wouldn't you? I guess they keep copying each other's mistakes. Anyway, when a character says, "Alert the Pentagon; raise our status from Defcon Four to Five" they're actually going the wrong way because Defcon One is the worst. Five is just the normal planetary levels of death and destruction.'

Distracted, I hadn't fully clocked how he was hanging back, running his hand across the top of a wall, so I'm not ready when a snowball comes flying. It hits me smack in the back. 'You utter bastard!' Some of it slivers down the side of my neck.

'Caught you napping at Defcon zero!'

I shovel snow with my hands, but he's faster on the draw and I come off worst again. It's a consolation when I manage to stuff some down the back of his shirt. I'm still celebrating when he asks, 'So what are these Defcon levels then?'

'Well – the lowest is blue, which is five. Then it goes green, yellow, red and up to white – which is nuclear bunker time.'

'That can't be right. For a start amber has to be in there somewhere.'

'It's not the same as traffic lights.'

'But the whole thing's perverse,' his voice is high with incredulity. At the crossing, there's nothing coming – no point in us waiting for the green man. 'Why not stick to a sequence that's internationally recognised? Everyone on earth knows red represents the most danger.'

'The Chinese believe red is lucky.'

'Okay, but what about blood?' he says. 'Or fire?'

'Fire would be lucky on a day like today,' I say. 'Wouldn't you rather be sitting in front of one right now?'

'Christ, wouldn't I just.'

I'm not sure how to take this, so I face it, him, head on. 'Listen, you've done your good deed. Thanks to you, I'm well fed, and it's been really good to get out of the hospital for a little while. Shouldn't you be heading off home now before this weather gets any worse?'

'No need, I've booked a room at The Montesquieu. We've stayed there before so they've given me one of their best rooms at their standard rate.' He looks very pleased with himself.

I can't think of anything to say except, 'How nice.'

'What's that supposed to mean?'

We've reached the main hospital entrance. 'Just that,' I say, 'nothing more.'

'With you it's never that simple.'

'Well today it is. Today, all I can manage is the obvious. Okay?'

'Sorry, Lottie. Wasn't thinking.' A snort of a laugh. 'Being my usual insensitive self.'

I take hold of his arm. 'I'd say the evidence suggests otherwise, Mr Warrington.' As we walk in, his cold hand fixes mine to the damp sleeve of his coat.

Bedside Manners

They've moved her to a higher floor. From this window's higher vantage point, I survey the world outside. Bleached of the usual colour, the city looks like an unfinished sketch. Since we got here the snow hasn't let up. It feels like the weather gods are toying with us. Very little is moving out there. In the various car parks surround the building, I can just make out the ghostly imprints left by lots of hurriedly departing cars.

Just a few degrees warmer and the rain would have run away quietly, instead everything is once again grinding to a halt. Mum was lucky her surgery went ahead before all this disruption. Everyday stuff isn't happening today. Somewhere in the building the telephone lines must be buzzing as they cancel all but essential operations.

Mum is still asleep, but she's been moving around more than she was earlier. Her breathing has settled into a quiet and melodic snore. Duncan and I have agreed several times that these are hopeful signs – not that either of us really knows.

I stare down at the city. The bedside tableau behind me is reflected in the glass. It looms massive against the office blocks and grand municipal buildings. If it weren't for the drip going into Mum's arm, the scene could be an old master painting with a title something like "The Bedside Vigil". I study Duncan's reflection, the way one of his hands is absentmindedly stroking Mum's forearm as you might a cat.

Fiddling with his mobile he says, 'I've just Googled those American Defcon levels.'

I turn on him. 'Shouldn't your phone be switched off?'

'I don't think that's a problem – not these days. Anyway, aside from the colours and number codes which you know all about, you'll never guess what the military call the highest level of alert.'

'Maximum alert level?'

He laughs. 'No.'

I turn back to face the view again and the snow stops falling like someone just turned off the machine. Studying the drooping clouds, I wonder if, or more likely when, they'll dump more of it on us. 'Come on, Lottie,' Duncan says, 'Guess again.'

'I give up – enlighten me.'

'Cocked Pistols! Bloody Cocked Pistols – like the last stand-off in a cowboy film before the big shoot-out begins.'

'Really?' I snort. 'Seriously – Bloody Cocked Pistols?'

'Well no – I mean, I added the bloody part; they're only cocked.'

'So that's alright then,' I say, my breath is misting the windowpane. 'And immediately after that comes the shoot-out – the big finale when dozens of mushroom clouds start popping up all over the world like fungi after rain.'

I watch him shake his head. 'You paint a lovely picture.'

A rim of brown scum borders the roads where they've thrown salt on them. I watch a tiny figure – can't tell the sex from this distance – trying to clear his or her front drive. It seems a futile battle so it's probably a man. The snow has just been turned on again. This time the flakes are bigger, closer together; this time they really mean business.

'Seriously though,' I say. 'You should switch off your phone in here, just in case.'

'You always were the cautious one. A worrier not a warrior.' He gets up and comes to stand behind me. I watch his mirror image as he says, 'What do you think might happen?'

'I don't know,' I tell him. 'Anything is possible.'

We were lying in bed one Sunday morning when Duncan asked me to marry him. Afterwards I wondered if he'd really meant to.

I'd woken up to the sound of him singing in the shower. Wearing only a towel, he was still humming when he brought me breakfast in bed. Coffee and toast. On the tray there was a handful of buttercups and daisies in danger of drowning in a mug. I realised he must have found them on the grass behind the bins.

I sat up, gulped down the coffee hoping it might help me feel a bit better. He handed me a piece of toast on a chipped plate; I could see the tramlines left where he'd scraped the burnt bits off. 'You can have anything on it beginning with marm,' he said.

I tapped the Marmite jar. When I removed the lid there was a crust of crumbs inside.

He picked up the almost empty marmalade jar. 'I might try the two together,' he said. 'Sweet and sour. Ying with yang. P'raps I should spread the Marmite on first.'

The toast was dry as cardboard and clogged my throat. I put my plate down and pulled up the duvet. I told him, 'I might actually be sick if you mix the two.'

'You know, Lottie, you need to be more open to new experiences,' he said.

I told him that eating disgusting combinations was hardly on a par with climbing in the Himalayas or rafting down some mighty river. In a high-pitched voice he repeated my own words back to me, '*I never get hangovers.*'

My head was hurting and I retreated under covers that still smelt of our bodies. When he carried on teasing me and I called him a prat, he pulled the covers from my head and waved the cup with the flowers in my face. 'Can't believe you called me a prat,' he said. 'Not after I brought you breakfast in bed with flowers.'

I snatched the cup off him, told him the poor things looked half-drowned. Then I held one under his chin. Seeing the golden reflection on his skin, I told him he liked butter.

'Yeah, sorry about that,' he said. 'It was rancid so I threw it out.'

I said I hadn't meant it literally and he shook his head and said, 'You've lost me.'

I found it hard to believe I needed to explain about holding a buttercup under someone's chin to see if they liked butter. 'You definitely like butter,' I told him.

He held another buttercup under my chin. 'This is a bit of

a crap game,' he said. 'It must be pretty boring up north if this constitutes fun.'

I complained he hadn't said whether I liked butter and he snorted. 'Do you need me to tell you?'

'Only what the buttercup said.'

'So is it a magic buttercup?' He made the flower dance in front of my face. 'Can it talk?'

I asked him if he'd smoked some of Nigel's grass after I'd gone to bed. He shrugged off the suggestion – told me he was just in a good mood. He turned the flower's head towards himself and said something about how grumpy I was.

I said he could be unbelievably annoying sometimes and that made him laugh out loud. I remember trying to whack him with my pillow, how he grabbed my wrists and said, 'Violence is the first resort of the feeble minded.' His grip was too firm for me to shake off.

Then abruptly he stopped laughing and began to kiss me. He tasted of coffee and burnt toast. I let the kiss take me, didn't expect him to break off when he did. His face so close it was a blur, he whispered, 'I want us to stay like this forever.'

'What, with just Marmite and marmalade and burnt toast to live off?'

'I'm serious,' he said. When he sat back a bit and I could see him more clearly, 'I want to live with you. Marry you, if you'd like to. Have kids together – all that stuff,' his expression was perfectly serious.

I asked him if he was proposing to me and he said, 'I think I must be.'

'This is a wind-up,' I said.

He insisted – said he might have been larking around earlier but not about the marriage thing – that he was serious about that. Then he spoilt it by adding, 'Deadly.'

I didn't know what to say so I said, 'Ask me again when I can be certain you mean it.'

That made him smile – a big Cheshire cat grin. 'Sounds like a yes to me,' he said. 'In principle, at any rate. I suppose I just need to work on my wooing technique.'

I can still see him sitting there. Through a gap in the curtains the morning sun was highlighting one side of his face; one eye was pale, luminous grey while the other one looked much darker.

Mum coughs, though it's more like a sneeze. 'Bless you,' I say, walking over to the bed.

Her eyes open a fraction. They're bloodshot around the edges. 'Lottie?'

Relief catches in my throat. 'Yes, it's me, Mum.'

'I can see that for meself.' She turns her head a fraction. 'Did I hear Duncan's voice just now?'

'I'm right here, Carol,' he tells her.

Her eyes light up after a fashion. 'Ah, I thought it was you.' There's no mistaking the fondness in her voice.

He says, 'How are you feeling?'

'Like I've been hit by a ruddy bus.' She's wheezing. She tries to raise her head, but finds it too hard. The wheezing turns into a series of coughs.

I'm not sure how to help. 'Would you like me to adjust the back of the bed?' I ask.

Her face screws itself into puzzlement: 'Just what?'

'Adjust.' I speak louder, slower. 'The back of the bed you're in moves up and down. I should be able to move it up a bit if I can find the right switch.' Looking at the control buttons, I'm nervous; I don't want to jolt her upright or tangle any of those vital tubes.

'Not too much.' Her breathing seems louder, laboured. 'You be careful our Lottie, I don't want you tipping me out onto the damn floor.'

Duncan's hand is on my shoulder, squeezing it. 'Why don't I ask one of the nurses to step in and take a look at her? They'll know what to do.'

He goes out and Mum and I are left alone. 'I'm so glad you're going to be alright, Mum,' I tell her. Her eyelids soon close again so I squeeze her hand to keep her with me. Her fingers give only the feeblest of responses. She smiles, a near toothless smile; then says, 'I know, it's …' Her fingers relax; the pressure is gone. Whatever she was about to say is too difficult for her right now; she's already fast asleep.

Past and Present

I watch over her. Very little outside noise intrudes through the glazing apart from for an occasional shrieking siren. Down below us the city is becoming paralyzed.

I have to bend over to hear the slight catch in Mum's throat when she breathes in. Aside from that, she appears to be sleeping peacefully.

It won't be easy for Duncan to find a nurse who is free. Earlier, they told us the hospital was operating with a skeleton staff; I'd had to suppress a smile at the surreal image that popped into my head.

I keep checking Mum's paper-thin eyelids for signs of movement but there are none. She's so still. There's little left of her old self – her once stout figure has been whittled down leaving too much skin and all her veins on show. The seed-head of hair resting on the pillow carries no remnant of its former colour. It's difficult to believe it was once jet black. She's lying on her back so it's hard to miss the impression of the skull that underlies her features.

She'd once been such a formidable woman – a force to be

reckoned with; Plump going towards fat in those broad-fitting sensible shoes. Always had a mass of wiry, dark hair. When I came along she was only thirty and yet I don't remember when it wasn't peppered with white at the front.

Every second week, Mum was on the early shift and so she was there when I got home from school. At secondary school, she was the first obstacle I would have to circumnavigate when I got in. I remember how she'd made me promise never, ever, to walk home by myself. 'You never know who's about,' Mum was over-fond of saying. At twelve going on thirteen, I'd begun to rail against the restrictions this imposed on my freedom.

The so-called Yorkshire Ripper had been the bogeyman haunting my early childhood. Hiding behind doors, I'd overheard tales of how he stalked the streets at night with a hammer in his hand. The threat of him meant every woman, including Mum, became reluctant to venture outside unaccompanied – especially at night.

'Peter Sutcliffe has been banged up for years,' I regularly reminded her. I didn't get why she remained so overprotective.

'Aye, well, there's plenty more like him about,' she'd say.

I usually countered that argument – and there were very many of those – by explaining how, statistically, this just wasn't the case. 'Mathematically, I'm far more likely to get hit by lightning than be abducted by some sicko.'

This proved an unpersuasive argument because Mum had a ready riposte about how Mrs Gardner, who lived in Carding Street, had been struck by lightning when it hit her umbrella. 'Half her clothes had melted clean away when they found her.'

She always relished this particular detail. Mum liked to finish on: 'The poor woman was never the same after that.'

One particular evening, I arrived home soaked through and furious because I'd had to wait for ages for Jasmine and Becky to finish netball practice. It was the summer term and broad daylight when I got out of school. Before Mum could say a word, I shouted at her – told her how, if I hadn't had to wait around, I would have avoided the rain and been home an hour ago.

She grabbed my shoulders, her immovable features far too close to mine. 'When will you realise it's not safe to be by yourself out there?'

'But *you* walk to and from the bus stop on your own every day. Why's it any safer for you than it is for me?'

This cut no ice. 'Them sort of men aren't interested in the likes of me,' she said. 'They're always on the lookout for pretty young girls.'

'You don't know that,' I told her. 'They might have a thing for older women.'

Dad's arrival ended round one of the argument. I went off to dry my hair and change. Inside I was still simmering.

Later, when I unpacked my school bag at the kitchen table, I discovered the letter from the school, which had been in the front pocket all week – a scuffed brown envelope with "Mr & Mrs H Preece" on the front.

I handed it to Dad. 'What's this then?' he asked. 'Not been skiving off school, have ya?'

I must have said something like, 'Thank you very much for your touching faith in me.' I'd been practicing a lot and sarcasm was my weapon of choice.

'So, what's all this about?' he asked.

'How the hell should I know?'

Dad ripped it open. His head moved back and forth with the words. Then, as if he hadn't just read it, he said, 'Parents' Consultation Evening? What's that about then?'

'*Well, some people's parents* are interested in how their children are getting on at school.'

Suspicion crossed his eyes. 'I thought you'd been getting good marks – them B pluses and A, something-or-others?'

'I have.'

'So what's all this about?'

'It's an opportunity to *actually talk* to my teachers, you know, face to face.'

He raised his voice so it would carry over to Mum. 'Says here we've to make an appointment with each of our Lottie's subject teachers about her choices for next year. Can't see the ruddy point. What the hell do either of us know about Chemistry or flamin' French?'

Looking worried, Mum came over to read the letter for herself. 'Oh, for Christ's sake,' I told them both, 'nobody's going to force either of you to go if you can't be arsed.'

'Language Charlotte!' As Mum read, her lips were actually moving.

Scratching the top of his head, Dad said, 'It starts at quarter-to-four – how am I supposed to get there by then?'

'Catch an earlier bus?' I suggested. 'Take an hour off? It's not that flaming difficult.'

'But I'd have to leave by three o'clock. They don't let you go early for no good reason, you know. It's got to be something important.'

'Don't bloody bother if it's all too much trouble.' I snatched the letter back and marched off up the stairs. I gave my bedroom door a satisfying slam before launching myself onto the bed.

Raised voices penetrated the floorboards. It didn't take long for their row to escalate; there was no such thing as a reasoned discussion in our household.

Sometime after it had finally gone quiet, there was a knock on my bedroom door. Mum's voice: 'Lottie love, I've brought you up a brew.'

I told her I wasn't thirsty but the door opened anyway and she came in holding the mug out like a peace offering. 'I'm on lates next week but I reckon – I'm pretty certain – I should be able to swap sifts with Muriel to get to this thing at your school. No need for your dad to have time off as well.'

Keeping my eyes on my book, I told her not to bother.

She put the mug down and reminded me to drink it while it was hot. 'It's not like we don't care, or owt,' she said. 'It's just you know far more about these things than the two of us put together. For me to get there on time – well, it hardly seems worth all the effort.' Her folded arms spoke volumes. 'Anyroad, I'll go if you'd like me to be there.'

Had it been Dad making the offer, I might have been more enthusiastic; I considered him marginally less embarrassing. I was always acutely aware of how ancient and old-fashioned they were compared to my friends' parents.

Once she'd gone, I spread out the form and ticked the box saying neither of them could attend. It was easy to forge Mum's signature at the bottom – I'd had plenty of practice.

The next night I told them they'd left it too late, that my teachers were all booked up now. That was the last time anyone in our house ever mentioned Parents' Evening.

Duncan comes back with a woman I presume is a nurse – I haven't cracked their uniform code.

'She's gone back to sleep now,' I say.

'Well, why don't I see how she's doing while I'm here?' They must practice that cheery voice. Duncan and I move to one side giving her more space to examine Mum. She's very thorough, dutifully records whatever it is she can tell from the various machines surrounding the bed. 'All done.' She gives me a fleeting smile. 'The consultant is due to see your mother later on today,' she says. 'He'll be able to tell you more than I can.'

Is she passing the buck? 'What time will that be?' I ask.

'As you can imagine, today he's a bit snowed under – excuse the pun.' She's smiling as she checks her watch. 'I expect it'll be five-thirty ish – possibly a bit later.'

Once she's gone, Duncan puts an arm round my shoulders. 'I think Carol's looking a bit better,' he says. 'There's more colour in her cheeks.'

To me she looks just as lifeless.

He squeezes my arm and says, 'I'm sure she'll be fine.'

'I'm not so certain,' I tell him. It's a small defeat when I rest my head on his chest.

'Why don't we go and get a cup of tea,' he says. 'My hotel's just around the corner, I'm sure they serve a decent brew – maybe they can throw in a cake or two. We can be back here well before five.'

I put on a smile. 'Afternoon tea with a married man at his hotel – what kind of floozy do you take me for?'

'The thirsty kind,' he says.

His laugh is a little too hearty. Even so, it doesn't take me long to give in.

Outside it's even colder than before; the glare from the lying snow hurts the back of my eyes like a hangover. I turn my collar up and blow on my hands though it has little effect. Beside me, Duncan seems to have shrunk down inside his coat like the Invisible Man. My feet are freezing; my shoes already soaked through. I'm slipping and sliding all over the place; several times I have to reach for him to stay upright and so we end up arm in arm.

The two of us fall into a comfortable rhythm – too comfortable. 'I don't want to sound ungrateful,' I tell him, 'but why did you come all the way up here?'

His face pinched in with cold, he stops walking and takes a deep breath, which he exhales in a cloud. 'I was there when you got that phone call,' he says. 'I could always read your poker face. It was obvious how shaken and worried you were. Knowing Kate was tied up with her exams, I guessed you'd play down the whole thing for her sake.' A twitch of a smile. 'Bottom line is, I wasn't going to stand by and let you face this on your own.'

I study his expression before deciding to take this explanation at face value.

Duncan says, 'What about your brother – shouldn't he be here?'

Kevin. The two of us haven't even spoken on the phone for more than a year – probably nearer two. I send him a birthday card if I remember and he just does Christmas cards. I once visited his house in Melbourne with my friends Zoë and Chris. It was years ago – the summer after we'd all graduated; just a brief stop on our trip around Australia and New Zealand. His place is in the St Kilda area – a pretty house, painted blue with a fancy ironwork veranda picked out in white. I remember the two of us sitting on it, listening to the racket of the parakeets.

Though they knew we were coming, Kevin and his wife seemed thrown off by our arrival. They did their duty, fed and housed us, but it proved a struggle to fill the growing gaps in the conversation. To say we have nothing in common is an understatement – there was far more separating me from my half-brother than the oceans that normally lay between us.

Taking out my phone, I say, 'I'll call him right now.'

'Are you sure? I mean isn't it the middle of the night over there?' Duncan looks at his watch. 'About three o'clock in the morning or thereabouts.'

'Too bad.' Am I doing this right now out of spite or necessity? Possibly it's both. I make the call anyway.

After a dozen or more rings someone picks up. A sleepy male voice says, 'What is it?'

'Hi. Is that Kevin?'

'Um, yeah, it is.'

I don't mean it when I say, 'Sorry to wake you,' before I add, 'It's Charlotte.' Stamping my feet to keep them warm, I choose not to fill the long silence with, 'your sister.' My breath clouds the air; powdery snow is flaking my coat like a bad case of dandruff.

Finally, he says, 'Has something happened?' I can't tell whether he's worked out it's me, or he's playing for time.

To keep warm I carry on walking. 'The thing is I'm phoning about Mum. She's not very well, I'm afraid.' In the photo he enclosed with his last Christmas card there was a definite meatiness about him; those broad shoulders were carrying a good many extra pounds. And a newly receding hairline gave his tanned face the confidence of a man who'd found his place in the world. Lined up behind him, his sons looked like they were in on the same joke.

'Oh right,' Kevin says. He makes me wait for, 'So what's wrong with the old gal?' His accent has grown more noticeable.

'She's in hospital. Things aren't looking very good.'

He yawns loudly. 'So it's serious?'

'Yes, it seems to be.' This is the first time I've admitted it to myself. 'She'd been getting really bad back pain, and you know, that she's, um, lost so much weight you wouldn't recognise her.'

'Let's face it, Charlie, I'd hardly recognise her if she hadn't. It's been almost fifteen years.'

'Anyway, they've operated on her, but, well, she's still looking pretty awful. She's very weak. To be honest, it could be really serious.' I refuse to say the words.

'But it might not be?' Another yawn. 'Isn't that what you're saying?'

'Look, I'm saying that it's probably very serious.' I can see where this is going but he's not going to make me decide for him. 'But I don't know that for sure. They haven't told us much – it's a question of wait and see.'

'So you're thinking maybe I should fly over? Only, right now's not the best time for me.'

'It's not the best time for Mum either.'

I'm caught out by his loud laugh. 'Yeah, I take your point, sis.' A heavy sigh. 'So when will they, the doctors, have a better idea?'

'I don't know – later today possibly. Listen, no one's forcing you to come, I just thought I should keep you informed. After all, the two of us are her next-of-kin.'

'Okay, Charlie, technically you're right but let's not kid ourselves. I mean, it's not like I don't care, but things are pretty tight for me here. These next couple of weeks could be, literally, life and death for my business – everything I've spent more than twenty years building up. I can't just up and leave – there would be consequences, believe me.'

'Then don't.' I'm tempted to cut him off at this point but I keep listening just in case.

'I might be able to make it in a couple of weeks – maybe by the beginning of next month. Best I can do right now, I'm afraid.'

'I'll say one thing for you, Kevin, you're consistent; you always were a total arsehole.' I hang up before he can respond.

'Glad you sugarcoated that,' Duncan says.

Tea for Two

As soon as we step inside the hotel, we're obliged to wipe our feet on the extra mats they've laid to prevent guests tracking snow onto the deep-piled carpet beyond. The lobby area is more or less deserted. There's a rope across the entrance to the restaurant; a handwritten notice tells us:

The dining room is regrettably closed due to the staff shortages resulting from the inclement weather.

Duncan approaches the bored-looking receptionist. He tells her his name and she checks the details on her screen. 'Ah – yes,' she says. 'I have you here. Your luggage has already been sent up, Mr Warrington.' The key she hands him isn't a card but a metal one with a wooden fob attached.

He gives her a winning smile then asks if someone could possibly rustle us up a pot of tea.

Whilst she goes off to enquire, we try to get comfortable in a couple of faux antique chairs. The change in temperature is making my cheeks feel like they've been in the sun. Soft music is playing – a muted, tinkling tune chosen to cause neither offence nor interest. I wonder they haven't swapped it for a snow themed medley. Scrolling through my emails, I start to hum. As soon as I realise the tune is *Baby it's Cold Outside* I stop.

Thankfully, Duncan's busy wrestling with a broadsheet newspaper that's had one of those wooden rods inserted in its spine. The receptionist interrupts his disgruntled muttering to inform him that they're still able to provide room service and she's ordered afternoon tea for two to be sent up.

Duncan unlocks "The Epicurus Suite". Stepping inside, he whistles. 'Wow, this is quite an upgrade.'

It's certainly really spacious. The furnishings are dark and heavy – mock fin de siècle. I go over to the window while he disappears through an inner doorway, presumably to pee. From where I'm standing I can just make out the main tower of the hospital blocks. Checking my phone, I find less time has elapsed than I'd imagined. No one has called me.

Duncan comes back with a couple of thick white towels. 'Catch!' He throws one in my direction. 'I think they must have mistaken me for someone else,' he says drying his hair. 'Some rich businessman.'

'Or an undercover hotel inspector.'

'Any minute now they'll discover I'm an imposter and start banging on the door.' Chuckling to himself, he drapes his towel over one shoulder like a waiter might and strolls around taking in the fresh flowers and complimentary wine beside the fruit basket.

'Lottie, come and look at the sheer size of this bed,' he shouts over his shoulder. 'What's bigger than King size? Is it an Emperor?'

I'm reluctant to enter the bedroom but it seems absurdly prudish to refuse. He's right – the bed's a monster. I laugh out loud. 'I believe that's the Bloody Dictator model.'

'Or possibly the Swingers' Special.'

'I wonder how they find big enough sheets for that thing?'

There's a knock on the outer door. Duncan goes to open it and I freeze. For a second, I imagine it might be his wife, Sarah. I'm relieved when it's only a waiter.

The man's uniform is royal blue with burgundy stripes down the trousers – designed to match the décor. He wheels in a trolley and parks it in the centre of the room. We watch him pick up two of the smaller chairs and carefully position them to allow us to sit facing each other.

As he leaves, Duncan slips a coin or two into his hand like you might a bribe.

The trolley is really a table on wheels covered by a starched white cloth and laden with gold-rimmed crockery. Highly polished silverware winks up at me. It's hard not to smile at the centrepiece – a tiered hierarchy of tiny sandwiches, mini cakes and dessert slices.

Duncan sits down, spreads a napkin on his lap and rubs his hands at the choice laid out before him.

I tell him I need to use the loo.

The bathroom is predictably huge with more marble than a mausoleum. Every sound I make echoes against the hard surfaces. Looking into the mirror, I notice how the snow has tousled my hair and reddened my cheeks in a way that suggests abandonment – the passionate type. Out loud I ask my reflection, 'What the hell are you playing at?'

I take a long breath before unbolting the door. 'Lottie, you have to try these sandwiches.' Duncan is waving something in the air. 'They're so far removed from anything you might normally eat.'

He pops the whole thing in his mouth at once. 'I'm pretty certain this one is ham.' Still chewing he says, 'There's a touch of horseradish in there. No wait – could be some sort of mustard.'

I sit down to face him. He's already poured the tea and so I take a long sip of mine. 'I'm not really hungry,' I tell him, though the truth is I'm tempted.

He scoffs. 'Look at the size of these things; they're hardly going to fill you up. Go on – try those ones with the pink filling before I finish the lot.'

'What's in them?'

'Definitely some kind of fish – salmon with dill would be my best guess.'

To please him I take a bite out of one; my teeth sink into salty nothingness. After that I try a green one. I can't tell what the hell I'm eating or decide whether it tastes good or bad.

'I thought those were cucumber or possibly avocado,' he says. 'Can you taste the chili?'

'Mmm.' I nod as the heat kicks in.

While I take small bites, he puts everything in his mouth at once. 'These red ones are a cross between a tart and a cake.' He swallows. 'A bit too sweet but still very tasty.' He takes another one.

'Hey – leave some for me,' I tell him. 'I plan to get to those when I've finished the sandwiches.'

'So you still refuse to mix sweet with savoury.' He waves his index finger in my face. 'You realise that's entirely down to early training, don't you?'

'Maybe, but I still prefer to savour the savoury stuff first.' I pick up what I take to be a tiny cheese scone. 'If you mix the two it only confuses the palate and spoils both.'

'Never tried sweet and sour pork? No cranberry sauce with your turkey?'

The scone is a little dry; probably not freshly made. I take my time chewing before I swallow. 'I suppose over the years I've learnt to make a few exceptions,' I tell him.

'That's a start,' he says. 'A small victory for decadency; old Epicurus would approve.'

This is play food; each new taste assaults my tongue leaving me surprisingly sated. Finally, I sit back, swallow the last of drop of tea and say, 'Thank you – that was delicious, I think. In any case I'm now utterly stuffed.'

Head on one side, he smirks – a look that's always suited him. I glimpse the giant bed through the doorway. For reasons I can't begin to explain, this seems the right time to mention something we've never spoken about – or more accurately I've never divulged.

'Did I ever tell you that my dad had an affair,' I say.

'No you most certainly did not!' He frowns. 'Are you quite certain because I must say, it–'

'I'm quite certain. He was careful to hide it. I only found out about by accident.'

Duncan wants to know everything all at once. 'Why didn't you tell me before? How did your mum react?' There's no disguising his rising excitement, 'So is that why the two of them were constantly arguing?'

I raise a hand. 'If you shut up for a minute, I might tell you.'

He pulls an imaginary zip across his lips.

'I know it for a fact because I saw the two of them together once. I'd gone to Leeds on the train. Dad and this younger, rather pretty woman – they were walking down a side-street arm in arm. The way he looked at her – it was just so obvious. I hid in a shop so they wouldn't see me and they walked on past.'

My hands keep folding and unfolding my napkin. 'Until then I had no idea – not the slightest suspicion. Afterwards, I began to notice the signs – things I would have previously missed. The careful lies he would tell Mum about where he was going or when he'd be back.'

'Bloody hell. So your dear old dad was a bit of a lad on the quiet.' Duncan shakes his head. 'Who would have thought?'

'I can tell he's gone up in your estimation.'

'No – that's not true. It's just that, you know, he's probably the last person I'd have expected to have some fancy woman on the side.'

'I'm not sure she was some *bit on the side* – just a little something to add a note of piquancy to his life.'

'I never said that.'

'That's what that phrase implies.'

Duncan sits back. 'I know where this is leading and, for your information, I don't see women in those terms. Not sweeties or honeys or … tarts – nearly missed the obvious. I've never used those words or thought like that, as you well know.'

It's obvious I've hit a nerve. I study the crumbs on my plate for a moment. 'Anyway,' I say, 'I think it was quite a serious relationship.'

He narrows his eyes. 'So you tried to understand why he was having this affair?'

'What's to understand? I could *surmise* that Mum wasn't enough for some reason. That he loved or fancied this other woman more. Perhaps my mum didn't understand him or maybe she understood him only too well.'

Eyebrows raised he says, 'Maybe Carol wasn't too keen on sex. Perhaps his mistress was more adventurous between the sheets?'

I shudder at the picture this conjures up. 'Who knows? And what's more, this is *my father* we're discussing, so I'd rather not go there.'

'Or it could have been a big mistake,' he says. 'Something he fell into and regretted almost immediately.'

'From the way he behaved, my guess is it probably went on for many years.'

'Oh.' He wipes his mouth, spreading a thin trail of strawberry or raspberry or whatever confection he'd been eating across his napkin. 'You didn't say it was a long-term thing. I guess that's different.'

'Is it?'

He drops the cloth on his plate and pushes the whole thing away. 'How the hell should I know? You told me nothing about it until just now.' His sigh is heavy, burdened. 'I know you and Michael recently split up, but other than that, I really know next to nothing about your life – your current life that is.'

When he leans back the light from the window narrows his pupils. 'I'm not doing so well playing the understanding friend, am I?'

I search his eyes for those flecks of green and they're still there, of course. 'You're here now,' I say. 'That counts for a lot.'

'But I'm not what you need right now.'

'Who says?' I lean over towards him; hesitate for a moment before I kiss him full on the lips.

Duncan freezes. Registering his lack of response, my mouth stops what it's doing. I'm about to apologise for my faux pas, for reading the situation all wrong, when his hand comes up and he strokes my hair.

We stand up. He grabs my wrist, pulls me to him. At first I try to disguise my need, but everything else in the world falls away, leaving no space for any pretense between us.

Wake Up Call

When I open my eyes, I find I'm staring up at a chandelier complete with artificial candles.

My euphoria evaporates. Turning my face away, I stop Duncan's hand – push it off my breast. 'This is wrong,' I tell him. 'We have to stop.'

Duncan groans. The two of us are sprawled out on the giant bed. 'Fuck,' he says. When he sits up, his hair is sticking up on end in a way I would normally find endearing.

'I need to get back to the hospital,' I tell him.

He rolls away from me. The vast bed between us, he stands up, scratching his head. I'm tempted to go round to his side and smooth his ruffled hair into place. 'This was a mistake,' I say averting my eyes from his. 'I'm sorry.'

I refasten my bra. Buttoning up my blouse to the neck, I say, 'It must be almost five.'

Duncan checks his watch. 'Ten to,' he says. 'There's still plenty of time.' He clears his throat. 'You're right though – we shouldn't. I mean we should get going.' He hops around instead of sitting down to put his shoes back on.

'You really don't have to come with me,' I tell him. 'I'm quite capable of managing by myself.'

At that he pulls a face. 'Just you try and stop me.'

The hospital looms up ahead of us, its red brick walls a beacon in this blanked out world. The warren of corridors is more or less empty; the lift comes as soon as I summon it.

"Tenth Floor. Doors opening."

We're back in the place where Mum was but she's not there. 'Where the hell have they taken her?' I cry. I'm starting to hyperventilate. Looking round at the other patients, I can see they are in no condition to face an interrogation.

Duncan grabs my shoulders. 'You need to calm down, Lottie!' He rests his forehead against mine. 'Look at me. There's bound to be a very simple explanation. She's probably having some test or a scan – something like that. Take a deep breath. That's it.' He looks around for reinforcements. 'Why don't we go and find someone who can tell us where she is?'

We retrace our steps. We're at the lifts when a nurse comes round the corner. I grab her arm. 'We're looking for my mother – Mrs Carol Preece – they've moved her. I don't know where she is or what's happened to her.'

She gives me a patient smile. 'I'm sure there's no need to worry – we're always shuffling patients around especially when we're busy and understaffed like today. The weather puts a strain on everything.'

'I bet,' Duncan says. He gives me a told-you-so look.

'Take a seat for a minute,' she says. 'I'll go and find out where she is.'

Turns out they'd moved her into one of the smaller side rooms on the floor below. I'm surprised and relieved to find Mum sitting up and awake. They've propped her more upright and raised the metal side rails. This time there are no machines around the bed – which has to be a good sign.

'Hi, Mum.'

Her eyes appear to take a moment to focus – to register us. She looks from Duncan and back to me and then nods her head a fraction. 'So where's our Katie then?' Without waiting for an answer, she says, 'Still at school, I 'spose.'

There's a raw edge to her voice. Perhaps that's from the operation – the tube they put down her throat. I notice her breathing is less regular than it was before but then she was asleep.

'Kate's nineteen now,' I tell her. 'She's away at university. Remember?'

I sit down beside her and put on a reassuring smile.

'Don't go… talking so soft.' She keeps coughing, is struggling for air in between breaths. Her weary eyes are swimming with tears. She turns to Duncan. 'All the ruddy nonsense our Lottie talks… Don't know how you… put up with her sometimes.' Her eyes flick between us. 'All that stuff she makes up… Scribbling away… I've told her… she needs to get out in the fresh… air more.'

'How are you feeling, Carol?' Duncan's voice is loud for her benefit.

'Bloody–' she swallows then tries again. 'Bloody awful.' Her mouth forms a bleak smile. 'Like ruddy death warmed up.'

Her skin has turned ashen 'You'll feel better soon,' I tell her as if I'm confident of it. I hold her hand and say, 'The operation is all over and done with now, Mum. It'll be the tube they put down your throat that's making it sore.' I spot a beaker with a spout – the sort Kate used to have. 'Would you like a sip of water?'

She shakes her head. 'Listen to me… for a ruddy change.' The effort forces her eyes closed. 'When I'm gone… I want you to burn all the lot ont.'

'Don't go talking like that, Mum, you're going to be absolutely fine from now on. If you want anything burnt, you'll be able to do it yourself.'

She's struggling to speak. 'I don't want you or anybody to go ferreting around… in my chest of drawers… and that… D'you hear me?' She has to rest before adding, 'Leave all them… things be… for once in your life.' A single tear emerges from one eye; I watch as it rolls down the creped skin on her cheek.

'Mum, honestly, there's nothing for you to worry about.'

Duncan gives me a look. He shakes his head. 'Don't go upsetting yourself, Carol.' His voice is too loud – too intrusive. 'She'll do exactly what you say – won't you, Lottie?'

'Yes, of course I will,' I tell her. 'Whatever you want, Mum.'

'That'll make a bloomin' change.' Her chuckle turns into a cough.

'In any case, it's not going to come to that.' I sniff back tears. 'D'you remember Dr Azziz – the surgeon? She told me they've managed to fix the problem you were having.'

Duncan says, 'That's right – the old plumbing's running as good as new.'

'You'll be up and about in no time,' I tell her.

She gives us a wan smile.

'Honestly, Mum, you'll be back home again before you can say boo to a goose, as Dad used to say.'

Mum turns her face away from me. Her eyes fall on Duncan and she says, 'You and me... we know different, don't we?' Raising her boney hand, she moves it very slowly towards her own face. She lifts her index finger in what I think is an attempt to tap the side of her nose but instead she points it directly at Duncan. 'Make sure you... look after my girls for me... when I'm gone.'

He nods several times. Voice thick with emotion, he says, 'Though they can look after themselves, you know. Kate is another tough old bird in the making. Can't imagine where they get that from, can you?'

Her throaty laugh mutates into more coughing. I can see the effort it's costing when she says, 'Aye, a match for any man... Always were... always will be.'

I need to do something, so I stand up. 'I'm going to see if I can find a doctor.'

Duncan presses my shoulder down, forcing me back into my chair. 'I'll go,' he says. 'You should stay here with your mum.'

I'm still holding her hand. Despite the cloying heat it's now icy. Her breathing begins to grow louder – frighteningly so. With those watery eyes focused on me, she tries to hold a smile before her mouth grows slack. Willing my voice steady, I say, 'You know how much I love you, don't you, Mum?'

A new note emanates from her throat – a low gargle. Her lips form the gentlest of smiles, 'Aye, I know that, lass... Never our trouble, was it?' The gaps between each breath grow longer. 'You were… always a little… devil… Would argue night… was ruddy day… if it suited you.'

It's a relief when Duncan comes back with the nurse we spoke to earlier. His face tells me more than I'm prepared for. Into my ear he says, 'I think maybe I should phone Kate at some point.'

Mum closes her eyes and mumbles, 'Going to be a chemist… that girl… or some such thing.'

Her breathing grows a little easier as she falls asleep.

'I've buzzed for the registrar,' the nurse tells us. She doesn't say why.

We wait for his arrival. I pray for some colour to return to Mum's cheeks, for her eyes to open again.

This time a different doctor walks in. Though Mum is asleep, he draws us aside. 'My name is Dr Hussain,' he says. 'I'm part of the team looking after your mother.' His expression is too grave for my liking. I look into his dark and doleful eyes and have to turn away. I'm overcome by a childish notion that if I anticipate what he's about to say, he won't say it, and then it can't come true.

'The results of your mother's latest blood test have confirmed what we suspected, I'm afraid.' He waits for me – for us – to take in the fact that this is not good news. 'The problem concerns your mother's kidney function.' He looks first at me and then at Duncan, to check we've fully understood. 'As you know, we successfully operated but, sadly, the blood loss must have disrupted the flow of blood to her renal arteries and, unfortunately, this in turn has caused the onset of renal failure.'

I know her death sentence is next. 'Regrettably, there's nothing more we can do for your mother except to keep her as comfortable as possible.' He holds up his empty hands and lets them fall away again. 'I'm very sorry – I wish it were otherwise.'

Final Acts

A primitive rasp builds up in her throat and without any words our shared look acknowledges what must be coming next. Should I summon a medic or maybe a priest to give her the last rites? It seems too late; besides, I recall her own often-expressed sentiment on the subject of belief: 'I don't hold much truck with *any* religion – caused more damn wars than anything else them men find to squabble over.'

Several times, Mum stops breathing only to suddenly start again. Her breath rattles in her chest every time it leaves her body – a horrible sound that builds and builds before it finally fades away.

And this time there is no inward breath.

I'm holding her hand and I look down at her motionless fingers. After a while, I decide I must let them go, and so I smooth her hand out on the bed sheet. My legs are shaking as I bend to kiss her cooling forehead and run my hand over her eyes, though they're already closed. 'Night night, Mum,' I say. 'Sleep tight.'

Duncan is weeping very loudly. The noise builds to a wail

that's so pervasive I want to block my ears to it. A nurse comes rushing in to investigate. She checks Mum over methodically, professionally, and then says, 'As I'm sure you've guessed, your mother has just passed,' like this is some test Mum's done well in.

Not died but passed – entered some other realm parallel to ours. The thought makes me glance up to the ceiling to check if her ghostly form might be hovering up there.

All I can see is a blank space.

I'm thankful the nurse doesn't buzz for anyone, doesn't intervene in any way to disturb Mum's well-earned rest. Instead the woman looks at me and nods in what I take to be an acknowledgement that this was Mum's time to leave us. In a low voice she says that, when we're ready, we might like to follow her to some dedicated grieving place – 'our bereavement suite' as she calls it, where we'll apparently be more comfortable.

I shake my head with some vigour. 'It won't help,' I tell her.

Duncan's still audibly sobbing. I more or less have to pull him to his feet so that I can lead him out of the building for the sake of those worried relatives still waiting on news of their own loved ones.

It's too late for us.

The freezing air hits my face like a slap; I welcome the shock. Duncan is unsteady on his feet. 'Sorry, Lottie,' he manages to say. 'This is the wrong way round. I just– ' His face collapses and he bends over like he might be throwing up, but instead he weeps uncontrollably. 'It's just, I know… oh Christ, I mean…'

He kicks at a nearby heap of snow like it's about to do him

harm. After that he calms down enough for me to lead him over to my car. I have to manoeuvre him into the passenger seat before I can get in myself.

In the glove compartment, I locate a small pack of tissues and hand him one. He blows his nose loudly a couple of times and then he grows quiet at long last.

We sit and stare out at the patterns superimposed on the world by the frosted screen. The glass looks like it has been colonised by ghostly ferns.

This isn't real – none of it. Events are entirely in my head – a vivid hallucination brought on by my over-fertile imagination. Mum was right – I should stop my silly scribbling and get out in the fresh air more.

It is really cold in the car; soon we're both shivering like cartoon characters. I shake the de-ice can and it sounds hollow; must be almost empty. I get out to spray what's left on the windscreen and manage to clear a big enough gap in the ice.

Back inside, I use a tissue to clear the corresponding area so that I can see well enough to drive the short distance to Duncan's hotel.

The traffic is light; everyone else has sensibly gone home for the night. I know the way now and it's not far. The back wheels skid at every turn. If we crash, then so be it; it's not in my hands anymore – nothing is.

At the hotel, we come under scrutiny from the same receptionist. She registers the state Duncan is in and, with a look of deep suspicion, hands over the damned key.

Upstairs, I lead him over to the couch and he slumps down.

I pour him a glass of the freebie water I find on the hospitality tray. There's also a bowl of untouched fruit but that seems less appropriate.

After a couple of gulps, he wipes his mouth with the back of his hand. 'I'm so sorry, Lottie.' He sniffs. 'Not trying to hijack your grief.' Then he pulls me down beside him and puts his arms around me. 'I'm so sorry, it's just – '

His tears wet my blouse; the hug we're in feels too hot, too close, and I shrug him off.

The minibar is disguised as an antique cabinet so it takes me a while to locate the damned thing. I grab a pack of peanuts and a couple of miniature bottles of whisky. Duncan shakes his head when I offer him one, so I pour both bottles into a glass and down the whole thing in a couple of gulps.

The heat sears my throat before it hits my stomach. It's hard to catch my breath. The taste in my mouth reminds me I don't especially like whisky. I shake out a handful of peanuts and shove the whole lot into my mouth. When I chew them, they taste only of earth.

I refill my glass with what promises to be fancy artisan gin and go over to the window where the snow keeps falling and falling on a continuous loop.

Needing to pee, I head for bathroom, glass in hand. While I'm sitting on the toilet, I study the many swirls and waves in the marble and wonder if they're the remnants of long dead plants or the last traces of tiny extinct creatures. I try to recall the three main types of rock but can only remember igneous and sedimentary. The third one eludes me.

After washing my hands, I splash some water on my face.

The me in the mirror looks the same as usual though I know for a fact she's not. I lurch, have to grab the edge of the bath for support. Being a lightweight these days, I'm definitely feeling the effects of the booze. But it's not enough – not by a long way.

Duncan hasn't moved so I simply ignore him and ransack the minibar trying to locate a teeny-weeny bottle of rum or whatever. I'm not fussy. Kneeling on the floor, I watch his legs approach while I sort through the booze I've covered the carpet with. There's another little bottle of artisan gin – it seems they come two-by-two like the animals in the arc.

'Changed my mind.' Duncan holds out a hand. 'I may as well join you.'

'Don't feel obliged,' I tell him. 'I'm perfectly happy drinking alone. In fact I'm used to it.' I can't find where I put my glass, so I swig a mini rum straight from the bottle. It goes down like medicine.

Duncan picks up its twin and pours the contents into a glass. 'How civilised,' I say, twisting the head off one of the bourbons. 'I think I might go for the vodka next. How about you – what do you fancy, Dunc?'

'Lottie, I mean it. I'm so sorry–'

'Sssh!' I lean over, put my finger to his lips and let it linger. 'No words – alright?'

'Whatever you say.' He pulls an imaginary zip across his mouth for the second time today and I think about how I'd like to run my tongue across his lips to taste the rum on them. And so I do it.

He's unresponsive – sits there like a statue. It's hard to

balance as I flip one shoe off. It bounces off the opposite wall. There's a thud when the other one lands somewhere behind me. 'You know what,' I say. 'After tonight, I'm done with stupid fucking words.'

It's hard to undo the buttons on my blouse. 'Talking of fucking.' Duncan is staring at me; his eyes are bloodshot and sad. Once the last button pops, I shrug it off.

Reaching for my hand, he tries to stop me from unfastening my bra. 'This isn't right, Lottie.'

'That's where you're wrong.' I escape his grasp and undo the hooks. Then I hold it up, swing it back and forth in front of his eyes like a hypnotist trying to put someone under. I throw the silly thing across the room and it lands on top of a lamp, which teeters before it rights itself.

Taking hold of both his hands, I place them on my breasts. 'This – this is right,' I tell him. 'Feels nice, doesn't it? Come on, Duncan. I mean, after all, isn't this what you came here for?'

'No.' He snatches his hands away. 'Not like this. Not when your mum has only just – '

'How about this then?' I grab his crotch through his trousers. 'Does this feel right?'

He shrinks from my touch. I give up and turn my attention back to my carpet minibar. 'D'you mind if I finish off the bourbon? Wait – why don't we send down for a whole bottle instead of this toy one?'

Duncan comes up behind, puts his arms around my waist and I feel the buttons on his coat push into my bare back, making contact with the full length of my spine. I swivel round in his arms and say, 'I know, let's raise a toast to our last night together.'

Hollow. No one is listening. All of this, everything has been left without a centre. Empty.

I'm empty.

Duncan is squeezing me so tightly, it's hard to breathe. He says, 'This is me, remember.' In my ear, like a whispered secret, 'You can let go.'

I push him away. 'What? Should I be showing more grief? Is that what's wrong?' I'm suddenly furious with him, with this stupid hotel suite, its opulent pretense that, for the right amount of money, you can be royalty for the night.

'Why can't they give people proper, grown up bottles?'

He shrugs.

'And in any case, who the hell drinks bloody bourbon up here in't north?' I weigh the offending miniature in my hand before hurling it across the room. It hits the giant television screen with a loud crack.

'Oh shit!' Leaning on the furniture, I go over to check on the damage. 'Oops – really sorry about that.' When I run my hands across the glass they catch on a dink the size of a stone chip. A couple of spidery cracks draw more attention to it. It looks like a child's sketch of a bullet hole, or possibly an arse-hole. I say, 'D'you think they'll make me pay for that? Could be an expensive mistake.'

Duncan says, 'Forget it. In the greater scheme of things, it doesn't matter.'

'Ah but it does. Look – there's an arsehole on the telly and it's not even switched on.' He isn't laughing. Concentrating on annunciating each word, I say, 'I realise I should not have done that. But you can't change things once they've happened, can you? That's it. They're done and fucking dusted.' My sight blurs. An unauthorised tear escapes. 'It's over,' I tell him. 'That's it – the flaming end.'

He keeps shaking his head. 'That may be true for your poor mum but not for you. You're only forty-six, Lottie. You have time to do anything you choose with the rest of your life.'

'But the best bits are over. The future's bound to be utter crap by comparison.'

His eyes soften. 'That's total bollocks, and you know it.' He takes his coat off.

'What, so you've changed your mind about the sex?'

He throws it on the couch, followed by his jumper. Then he starts unbuttoning his collar and the front of his shirt.

I manage a smile of sorts. 'Tempting though it may be – *you* may be – I have to tell you, Mr Warrington, that my previous fucking offer has just expired.'

'Forget all that nonsense.' He drapes his shirt around my shoulders, crosses the arms to wrap me in it like I'm suffering from exposure.

Stripped to the waist and still a fine figure of a man – as Mum would say. 'Please, Lottie,' he says, 'let's just hold each other.'

Aftermath

I think I managed to doze for an hour or two and then again for a little while longer. In any case, we're both fully awake by four so we talk and then just hold each other. Grief hits me in successive waves and I cling to Duncan, wetting his chest and both our faces with tears and snot. He envelops me in warmth and tender words. 'I love you so much,' he whispers into my hair as he strokes it.

Because it's the honest truth, I say, 'It's always been you. No one else has ever come close.'

After a while I fall asleep again.

The pain in my head wakes me. My mouth is a sandpit. Opening my swollen eyelids, I'm utterly drained after a night of conflicting emotions. The bedside clock shows it's 6:21. I slip out of bed and head for the toilet. The room sways under me like I'm onboard a ship. The bathroom is an echo chamber that intensifies every sound I make. When I'm done, I take a bathrobe off its hanger and pull it on. It's man-sized – way too big and bulky.

The thought of the day to come makes me feel wretched in so many ways I can't fix. In the main room, the carpet is a minefield of miniature bottles I have to negotiate. Reaching the depleted minibar, I take out a bottle of water and gulp most of it down.

Duncan hasn't stirred. After considering the alternatives, I climb back into bed beside him. I nestle up close and luxuriate in the warmth of his body against mine. His distinctive smell is a memory I'd almost forgotten though I'd recognise it blindfold. As I watch him sleep, I warm my cold feet against his legs like I used to.

Outside the snowbound city might still be sleeping. No light penetrates the heavy curtains. Aside from Duncan's steady breathing no noise infiltrates the walls that surround us. For this moment we can lie together peacefully in our bubble world.

It was years ago, too many to count, yet the memory conjures up a burnt ochre residue – the scent of stale beer and old wood in *that* pub.

I knew the place so well; we hung out there sometimes twice a week or more for three years. Its name has momentarily escaped me. "The *two-syllable* Arms"; something archaic: Miller's? Cooper's? It won't come. I can still picture that foot-polished floor, feel my hair brushing against the low-hanging beam with its hackneyed "duck or grouse" sign.

On the day in question, I was sitting in a draughty window seat near the main entrance. With only half a bitter for company, my eyes kept skimming the same passage in my book. A group of loud lads who had to be students had been gradually shifting until they blocked my view of the door. Damn. The sickly smell of dope began to circulate; smoke hung around them though it wasn't clear who was smoking it. Heads were nodding to the music, which might be *Black Magic Woman* – the Santana version. They looked like Muppets.

'*Never wait more than five minutes,*' Sal was always saying. '*You need to make sure you start as you mean to go on.*'

It had been almost fifteen minutes and I knew I really ought to leave. I'd got stacks of work waiting but each time there was a new draught from the door, I craned my head round a mass of buttocks and hoped it was him. When he finally appeared, I was both relieved and annoyed. Damn it – he looked so good it was hard to be angry.

Fast-forward two hours and the music had mellowed a bit, nothing as cool as moody jazz; more like some Oasis track. Two sets of empty glasses and us balancing matching beer mats on the edge of the table trying to flick backwards somersaults. He was concentrating hard on the next flip; his fringe hung down obscuring the top half of his face. I noticed the way his jaw set when he concentrated, the delicate movements of his hands as he kept repositioning the mat, getting the balance right.

Next second it was spinning up and away from the table to land more or less back where it started. He raised a triumphant fist in the air and shouted, 'See that? A triple somersault!'

The forty-somethings at the next table turned with disapproving stares; he didn't appear to notice their stopped conversations.

'No way,' I told him. 'Two at most.'

'Must have been too fast for you to see.' He leant towards me, a challenge in his eyes. It was hard to decide on their colour – I never could. 'You're not going to be a sore loser, are you?' They appeared greenish grey in that light on that day.

The beer mat in front of me was a bit bent, so I slid a new one across. It was yellow and red, a different brand; weighing it in my palm, it seemed a bit lighter. I said, 'Sit back and watch an expert at work,' while trying to get the over-hang just right.

It was all in the balance and I was ready.

My fingertips hit the edge of the table as it shot off to land on the floor some distance away. His full-volume laugh turned more heads. When he leant right down to retrieve it, I studied the contours of him – tried to picture the stripped-down torso inside that bulky navy jumper.

He handed me back my dust-covered, sorry-looking beer mat. 'Impressive technique,' he said.

Straightening it out, I told him, 'Watch and learn.' Couldn't stifle a smile.

'Another drink?' He stood up and I found myself staring directly at the crotch of his faded jeans, 'What would you like?' he asked me. I looked up into his face; no, he hadn't noticed.

'Beer, just a half. Oh, and some plain crisps. No, make that a packet of peanuts – I'll pay.'

'My round. What kind of nuts do you like?'

He was teasing me – he'd noticed alright.

'The regular sort,' I told him.

As he walked up to the bar, I followed his movements like a camera. He walked the line well.

He was back inside five minutes; I guessed that black-eyed barmaid must have picked him out in the crowd.

'If you're willing to learn from a master.' With care, he moved our glasses, then shifted his chair round so he was sitting beside me. 'You see, it's all in… how can I put this? Let's say the delicate balance between mat and man.' Up close, his mouth was fighting to stay serious. 'Or mat and woman, in this case. You need to find that Zen moment just before the flip. Here – let me show you.'

He positioned the beer mat with care and I smelt the softness of his newly shaved face, the beer on his breath, the warm closeness he promised. He picked up my hand and placed it below the overhang, straightening the tips of my fingers one by one, then squeezing them gently together to form a blunt edge. 'Now shut your eyes.'

'Don't be daft, I – ' The hand on my forehead silenced me as it swept down to close my eyes.

'Trust me. Okay, you've got to keep them shut. And now repeat after me: I am the beer mat.'

I was giggling too much, but he was waiting so I straightened out my mouth and said, 'I am the beer mat.'

'Good. I am the air it travels on.' His voice was deep and serious.

I repeated in a spooky voice, 'I am the air.'

'Concentrate.' His hand left my shoulder. 'Okay, it's up to you now. Feel the balance, Lottie. Only you, you must choose the exact moment.'

I waited.

My fingers hit the table hard and it hurt. I opened my eyes and the beer mat was exactly where it had been only now it was swimming in a pool of beer.

But Duncan wasn't concerned with the mess; he held both hands up and then brought them together in a loud clap. 'Perfect.' He clapped some more and nodded at me in acknowledgement. 'I made that a double backward flip, with a forward twist. You're the winner, Lottie.'

Ignoring the beer dripping onto the floor, I half-stood to make a mock bow. 'What can I say, talent will out.' In that moment I almost believed it.

'Exactly right.' He picked up his sticky drink and raised it in salute. I sat back down and did the same. Our wet glasses chinked together.

Right beside me, his breath on me, his lips just skimming my ear, he said, 'Remember, Charlotte, *you* choose the moment.'

If I had a handy time machine, I'd choose The Wheelwright's Arms, Shepherd's Bush, the evening of the February 27th 1992.

Morning is Broken

The trouble with bubbles is that as soon as they come into contact with any sharp object, they burst.

Duncan groans then sits upright with a jolt. His first words are, 'Christ – how did life get so fucking complicated?'

It's hard to think of an answer to that.

After rubbing his eyes, he gets out of bed and heads for the bathroom. He's in there for some time. When he comes out, he's wearing a dressing gown. Without a word, he walks past the bed and into the main room.

I lie back and close my eyes, try to shut out the lights he's put on. A little while later, phone in hand, he reappears in the doorway. 'I sent a text to Sarah after you fell asleep last night.' He's the very picture of guilt. 'I explained the main roads were shut – which is true. Anyway, I just sent her another text telling her I'm likely to be stuck here for a while longer.'

The words *stuck here* lodge in my brain. I say, 'Why send a text? Shouldn't you have spoken to her?'

'I couldn't. Still can't.' He runs a hand over his mouth. 'It sounds cowardly but I don't trust my voice not to betray – well, you know.'

'As far as I recall nothing happened last night; nothing physical that is.'

'You call that nothing?' He scoffs. 'I don't expect to be let off on a technicality.'

'Okay.'

'What does that mean?'

'I have no idea. I'm lost.'

He sighs, comes over and puts his arm around me. I try to stop myself from weeping but it's impossible. He rubs the top of my arm until it begins to feel sore. 'Your mum was a remarkable woman,' he says. 'Sure, some sad things happened to her but there was a lot of good stuff too.'

'I suppose so.'

'You're one of them,' he says. 'The two of you may not always have seen eye to eye but she adored you. And our Kate, of course.'

'And you.' I sniff. 'I remember she took to you right away. Said she thought of you as a son.' My nose is running and I haven't got a hanky. I think, what the hell and wipe it on the pristine sleeve of my dressing gown. 'Not that her real son is much of a rival.'

I look straight up into his broad, tanned face, into the very centres of his grey green eyes, the dark spheres that are trained on me. It's tempting to say so much, but where would I start?

His brow furrows. 'So, what are we going to do about Kate?'

'Oh, Christ, what are we going to do? I mean I have to tell her, I should have done it last night.'

'I've thought about ringing her myself,' he says. 'But what the hell's she supposed to do, poor girl? Nothing's moving out there – she can't get here at the moment even if she wanted to. Besides, what's it going achieve to upset her when she needs to stay calm for that final exam?'

'Are you seriously suggesting we keep this from her?' I sit up. 'That we wait until this evening before we tell her that her granny died yesterday?'

'It's only a few more hours. I agree it sounds shitty, but can you think of a better plan?'

Shaking my head only makes the room spin. 'I can't think,' I say. 'That's the trouble – my brain's frozen.'

'Look, for a start why don't I get some coffee sent up?' He picks up the receiver by the bed. 'And you should eat something – we both need to eat. We've had nothing since yesterday teatime.'

'You want me to think about food at a time like this?'

As if on cue, his belly rumbles. 'Hear that?' he says. 'Basic biology – the need for sustenance.' He looks at me expectantly. 'Come on, Lottie, you must be hungry; what takes your fancy?'

His hand hovers above the buttons.

'Now you mention it, I'd kill for a coffee.'

'Okay, good start. How about some croissants? Do you still like those almond ones?'

'Plain will do.'

'I'll see if they can bring us a selection. Maybe some orange juice and toast – oh, and some muesli as well.'

'Whatever – I really don't mind.'

'Breakfast is the first step,' he says. 'Let's worry about the next after we've eaten.'

In the Moment

There must be at least 30 centimetres of lying snow outside, while in here, in our fancy suite, we're sitting up in bed eating a continental breakfast in continental temperatures, both of us bulked out like snowmen in hotel dressing gowns.

I'm trying not to think of anything but the croissant on the plate in front of me and whether I should put more butter on before spreading it with strawberry jam. I glance across to Duncan. I'd forgotten his habit of putting a vast quantity of jam and butter on the side of his plate and preparing each individual mouthful at a time.

The events of yesterday could almost be a fever dream; my brain's not ready to process any of it. All the same my eyes water and so I stare down at the crumbs on my plate and wait for the world to become clear again.

Mindfulness is supposed to be a way of quieting your thoughts. Focusing on the present, what's occurring now and ignoring everything else. I've tried it a few times without a great deal of success. My mind refuses to cooperate; I can't stop it straying off to wherever it sees fit to wander.

Zoë was always a big advocate of the importance of staying fully present in the moment. 'You need to cultivate an attitude that's non-judgmental,' she was fond of telling me. Whenever I think about Zoë, I picture her sitting cross-legged on a rug in a festival field, head angled towards the sun, eyes shut as she communes with nature.

Hard to believe it's been so long since last I saw Zoë in person. Before that particular weekend fifteen years ago, everything in my life had seemed settled. On my way over to Duncan's, I'd been sure that, with the exception of Kate, the connection between him and me had been eroded like a bridge that can no longer bear any weight. And after all it had been six months and two weeks since our marriage had been officially declared over. The Decree Absolute certificate was sitting in the drawer of my desk along with various other awards.

I recall being behind the wheel on a road signposted *Chiswick and M4*, which could just as easily read: *to a new and fulfilling life*. It was a sunny day and I was happy as I pulled into the layby next to his house to drop Katie off for the weekend. I was planning to swap *The Twits* for Beyoncé at maximum volume.

Duncan came to the door in jeans and a jumper, wearing no shoes. He was holding a mug of coffee. He didn't say anything much, and I could see from the unruliness of his hair that he'd probably just got up. Yet as Katie let go of my hand, I felt this overwhelming sensation that every tiny little thing about him was how it ought to be. The way he held that cup, the way he put it down to lift our daughter and start her squeals of laughter – all of it was exactly right. And then there was the way he smiled down at me without saying a word.

Remembering his manners, he invited me in – asked me if I wanted a cup of that great smelling coffee. On the threshold, I hesitated.

What if I hadn't? What if at the end of our funny, awkward conversation, I'd admitted it right back then? Said something like, *I think we might have made a really big mistake*? Or *I realise now I've been wrong about a lot of things.*

Instead I shook my head and said, 'Well, I better be off. I'll be back around seven-thirty tomorrow, if that's okay?'

And he said, 'Fine by me. Kate, say bye to Mummy.'

She'd given me a quick hug before running into the house. Duncan and I said goodbye and that was it.

For a good five minutes I stood on the narrow pavement looking at his closed door, while the traffic revolved around me. I was tempted to knock again, ditch the plans I'd made and tell him exactly how I was feeling.

Instead, I drove on autopilot to the Womad Festival where I met up as planned with some old friends from uni.

Leaving behind Jane Margaret, my friend had rechristened herself the previous year – reinvented herself as the less conventional Zoë. I noticed the white in the roots of her radish-red hair. She might have passed for late twenties in the right light though not out in the open on a bright day.

She'd made a head start on the dope. My sober eyes kept returning to that blanched out parting of hers. People came and went around us as we sat on the damp grass and tried to ignore Chris and Flynn who were arguing about the merits of one of the acts. The lads kept forgetting to turn the burgers and the sweetcorn wrapped in its singed leaves.

I needed to talk through what had happened and so I told Zoë how I'd felt seeing Duncan again. Using her wise-woman voice, she said, 'That's what I like to call a *tremotion*. Don't worry, it will pass.'

'That's not even a proper word.'

She took a toke – made me wait for a response. 'It may not be an exact translation, I admit.'

'Of what, exactly? I mean, you can't simply make one of your usual pronouncements and then not explain. What does it mean, this *tremolten*?'

'You know, Lottie, you seem pretty strung out these days.' She took a longer toke. 'And the word is tre-*motion*; an Indian concept.'

'Oh right – so which particular Indians are we talking about here? The Indians in India, or in North America or South America?'

The tiny diamond in her nose caught the light. 'Everything has to be so pacific for you, doesn't it?'

I restrained from correcting her English.

'Anyway,' she said, 'what the fuck does it matter? It's the idea, the concept, that counts.'

Smoke from the barbecue was beginning to sting my eyes. 'Okay, then what's the concept?'

'Hard to explain really *precisely*. If you start jumping down my throat, I won't even bother.'

'Fine.' I held up both hands in submission.

'Okay, well, the idea is there are many different paths we

can take in life. We often don't notice when we're choosing. You know, you might be thinking: should I put butter on my sweetcorn? Or should I go to the toilet once the queues have gone down a bit, or just piss in the next field? Those sort of things.'

She paused to swat at a wasp, watched it circle around and then head off towards our dirty glasses. 'And then there's the bigger ones,' she said, 'like should I see the whole of this act and miss the acoustics in the Siam tent? Or should I sleep with Flynn just because I fancy a shag and I'm stoned?' Her hands weighed imaginary weights. 'I'm thinking yes to both by the way.'

She leant forward for the next bit. 'Then there are the really big ones like: should I move to Mexico or become a lesbian?' She wagged a finger in my face. 'Those are the ones that really change your pathway.'

'Okay, so, worryingly, I'm following your thread here Zoë, but I'm not sure where it's leading.'

'I'm getting there. Like I was saying, decisions lead you to different pathways and some are small and some are big. For you, getting divorced was a big one, right?'

'Of course.'

'If you hadn't divorced Duncan your life would be different now. You might not be sitting in this field today, for example. Anyway, sometimes there's like a... Well, it's like that idea of a rip in the space-time fabric. You know, those wormholes that people can drop through and end up in a parallel universe, or a distant galaxy or whatever.'

'Okay that sort of makes sense,' I told her. Perhaps the smoke from her joint was affecting me.

'It's not an exact analogy,' she said. 'But this morning you experienced a vibration from the old pathway you were on. Oh, and you have to remember we're talking about your inner being. Your emotions can lag behind or get speeded up – or should that be sped up? Anyway – today they were out of sync. You were having a *tremotion* – your emotional response wasn't in time with the pathway you're now on.'

'So, you've just mixed the word *tremor*, with the word *emotion*, to describe this.'

'Or someone else did.' She shrugged. 'Can't remember now. It could be *tremble* and *motion*. Doesn't actually matter what you call it – it's a well-known thing.'

Her theory seemed to make perfect sense. 'So, what you're saying is that my wanting to still be with Duncan is due to my emotional state lagging behind reality, and it will soon play catch up.'

She waved that knowing finger. 'Exactly. You just have to hang around for a bit until it does.' I looked over to where the burgers were now spitting flames. 'And here's my personal contribution to the theory,' she said. 'I reckon you might be able to speed the process up at times.'

She offered me the joint and, though I've always hated the smell, I took a toke. 'How, exactly?'

'Think back over the things that made you hate him in the first place.'

'I never *hated* him. We just weren't getting along.'

Zoë knitted her eyebrows in concentration. 'What about the things that really annoyed you? The hurtful things he said. Or the stupid, selfish, useless things he did.'

'Like what?'

'What, you can't think of a great long list of them?'

'Not many.'

Her dilated pupils came very close to me. 'That could be a bit of a problem.' She reached out to take back the joint then drew on the cardboard roach – all that was left. 'In that case you could try my own personal fail-safe solution.'

'Let me guess, I should shag Flynn.'

'Works for me every time.'

'What is it?' Head on one side, Duncan is looking at me.

'Sorry?'

'You laughed.'

'Did I?' I swallowed a mouthful of croissant. 'It was nothing – I was thinking about Zoë. D'you remember her?'

'What that tie-dyed-in-the-wool friend of yours from uni?'

'The same.'

'Whatever happened to her?'

'She's living in Peru at the moment.' I spoon more jam onto what's left of my croissant.

'Wow, well good for her,' he says. 'I never told you this but she once made a pass at me. A very awkward one, I have to say.'

'Only once?'

'I didn't realise she was a man-eater.'

'Not just men.'

He sits up. 'Really? You never told me that before.'

'Look at you; all perked up. I'm certainly not going into detail about her numerous sexploits.'

'Why not? It can't matter if she's living in Lima or wherever.'

'Actually, she's in Arequipa.'

'Same principal I would have thought.'

'Some things need to remain private between friends.' I laugh out loud at his expression. 'Not in that way, you idiot.'

His face grows sombre. 'Maybe that's always been our problem – too many things left unsaid.'

I sip my coffee. It's strong – too bitter without sugar.

'For example,' Duncan clears his throat, 'why didn't you tell me before about your dad having a mistress? You must have been utterly devastated when you found out.'

I shrug. 'There wasn't much to tell.' I stir in just a half a spoonful, avoid his eye so he can't accuse me of lying. He's always been damned nosey, eager to hear about other people's secrets.

The thing I've learnt about secrets is that they focus such destructive energy; in some circumstances they can turn you into your own blackmailer.

Next Steps

As if grief has made me an invalid, Duncan insists on clearing away the breakfast things. He puts the tray outside the door for some unseen lackey to whisk away. 'Right, I'm going to take a shower,' he says and disappears into the bathroom. After a few seconds I hear the water running.

Earlier, I had pulled back the heavy curtains and daylight is seeping in through the sheer fabric designed to hide us from prying eyes. I stretch out, lie right back on the pillow to take in the whole baroque nonsense of this place. Maroon and purple drapes hang in pleats from the ornate coronate above my head; the colours tinge the skin on my arms; I hold them up and they look almost corpse-like. For a moment I entertain the idea that everything is the other way round and this is *my* dying fantasy. Sadness could overwhelm me if I let it. Remembering half learnt mindfulness techniques, I concentrate only on my breathing, try to empty my mind of everything but the sensation of lying on this bed in this moment.

A sound breaks the spell. I get that primal sensation of being watched. I'm right; Duncan is out of the shower and standing a few metres away with a towel wrapped around his waist. Without my lenses he could be any of the ages I've known him.

His wet hair is plastered to his head, otter style. He says, 'It's a great shower – it's got these side jets that massage you from every angle. Very invigorating.' Though I can't see beneath the towel, from the gap at the side it looks like his tan is all over. He's not the sunbed type so they must have been on a beach holiday recently.

I run my hand over the smooth and sumptuous sheets and wonder if anyone is ever taken in by this whole fantasy of entitlement. 'I should get up,' I say.

'There's no rush.'

'I really ought to start phoning people – breaking the news and all that.' Getting out of bed, I'm careful to keep my distance from him.

'I could do some of that if you like. What about your brother? Given your last conversation, I'd be happy to phone him if you'd rather not speak to him right now.'

'Thanks but I should be the one to phone Kevin. However, first things first – I have to phone Kate.'

'You're sure? I mean you don't think it would be better to put it off until later?'

I hold up my hands. 'How much later? This evening? Tomorrow morning? There's never going to be a right time to tell her. Besides, I'm sure her uni will make allowances under the circumstances.'

'I take your point. Yes, I'm sure they will.' Practically naked, he comes towards me and presses his damp forehead against mine. 'Would you rather I did it?'

I force myself to break away. 'No – I think it should be me.'

My clothes have found many and varied resting places. The tale they suggest is far more debauched than the reality of what happened yesterday. I gather them up – leave them in an altogether more respectable pile. Duncan hands over a shoe.

Even as I select "Kate mob" I know for certain everything is wrong about this, but there's no choice; I have to do it.

She answers after three rings: 'Hi, Mum.' So casual and off-guard. When I start to tell her, it feels like a barrier inserts itself between my words and what I'm trying to say, and between us both and what's actually happened; and though I try my best, it feels like it's growing more impenetrable the longer I talk.

At first Kate is silent. Then comes a torrent I daren't interrupt. She goes quiet again; there's music in the background so I know she hasn't hung up. Between sobs she says, 'I'm sorry, Mum... I didn't mean to say those things... it's – '

We cry together. I feel her pain in my chest. In a quiet voice she says, 'I'll call you back.' Then she's gone.

What did I think would happen? Duncan might have been right about waiting, but it's done now and can't be altered. He asks me how it went, tries to comfort me but I grab my clothes and tell him I'm going to take a shower.

I lock the door behind me and lean against it.

Making sure my mobile's within arm's length, I undress, turn on the shower and step into it. Water jets assault me from all directions, pummelling and prying into every part of my body. There's a symbol for what looks like downpour mode. I turn the dial, turn up the pressure and water pounds down on my head and shoulders. My skin turns red, my fingertips grow pale and wrinkly, but I let it go on and on until Duncan bangs on the door and asks if I'm alright.

I turn off the water. 'Yes, I'm fine,' though I'm far from it.

I wrap a towel around my head. The last vestige of my makeup has washed off. My clothes could be fresher but I can't pretend to care. Fully dressed, I shake my hair out. With no comb, I rake my hands through getting the worst of the tangles out. Then I take a deep breath and unlock the door.

The phone in my hand rings and I'm so relieved that it's Kate. This time she sounds a little more controlled. It seems a housemate has dosed her with sweet tea and confirmed what I told her about not being able to get here. She's going to check the trains again later. 'I suppose there's no rush,' she says. 'Not now anyway.'

'I love you so much,' I tell her before she hangs up again.

I'm so thankful to this friend of hers – some girl called Freya whom I've never even met. If only I could fly the distance between us and put my arms around her. If only we were part of a bigger, closer family going through this loss together.

Duncan is talking on the phone to someone – I guess it's probably Sarah. I sit down on the crumpled bed and wait for him to finish. Outside the snowflakes are smaller than they were – the Eskimos must have a better word than powdery.

I press my forehead against the cold glass and stare out at the newly transformed city – a blank sheet; our own tabula rasa. If only. Though the buildings vary in style and size, they're all caught up together in a cat's cradle of drooping wires. Not much is moving apart from a snow plough and a few bent over pedestrians.

It's gone quiet in the other room. Through the gap in the door, I spy Duncan sitting on the couch flicking through a magazine. He's dressed in the same cord trousers. His sweater is thicker and light grey. It suits him.

He stands up when I come in and exhales long and loud. 'Why don't we get out of here,' he says. 'Don't know about you but I could really do with some fresh air.'

His hair's messier than it was – perhaps he forgot to pack a comb. He's slicked it back at the front after a fashion but it doesn't look as if it's going to stay put for long.

I say, 'I'm not sure my shoes are up to the conditions out there.'

His smile is trying hard: 'You could put a pair of my socks over them.'

'Does that really work?'

'So I'm told. We can but try.' He goes through into the bedroom and I watch him kneel before his suitcase. He throws each unwanted item over his shoulder until half his things are spread out over the mock Turkish rug. When he comes back, he's holding two grey woolly socks at arm's length. He gives a little bow and says, 'For you, madam.'

'Are you sure this is going to work?'

He shrugs. 'Might as well give it a go. Bound to be easier than carrying you over my shoulder in a fireman's lift.'

'Always been one of my fantasies,' I tell him.

He laughs and says, 'I'm not sure my back's up to it these days.'

It's quite a struggle to get the socks over my shoes but I manage it in the end. Once they're on, I parade my elephantine feet in front of him. 'I think they lend you an air of sophistication,' he tells me.

We venture outside arm in arm. The pavements are thick with compacted ice. We slip less often if we keep moving forward. Besides us the snow ploughs have cleared a single carriageway in each direction but a resistant layer of slush remains. Tons of greying snow has been piled up by the machine either side of the roadway.

There's very little traffic. A few 4x4s pass us with smug looking drivers at the wheel. I'm not sure either of us knows where the hell we're going. We trudge on, neither of us speaking. Despite being physically close, I sense a new awkwardness between us. In the great British tradition, I end up remarking on the weather and the decorative qualities of snow.

He doesn't respond. Some way up ahead of us a stout man is gingerly picking his way towards us with a tiny, brown and white dog on a lead; most of his face is hidden by a bright red scarf.

Steadying me at the crossing, Duncan says, 'So tell me about Kate – just how badly did she take it?'

'She was totally distraught – there's no other word.'

'I bet.' He pulls a pained expression.

'The worst part was how angry she was with me.' I grab hold of the freezing lamppost for support but when it starts to hurt, I let go again. 'She kept saying I should have told her how serious Mum's operation was; that I'd effectively robbed her of the chance to say goodbye to her granny. I tried to explain that I hadn't expected Mum to die but she wouldn't…'

'She won't have meant it – not really.' The weight of his arm is around my shoulder. 'That's just the grief talking.'

I lean in closer; his jacket against my cheek is a rough reminder of all the other times when we walked together like this. 'She outright accused me of lying to her.'

His voice cracks a little when he says, 'I wish you'd let me make the call.'

'She's right though, isn't she? I shouldn't have played down Mum's operation. I ought to have warned Kate that it might be serious.'

'Hindsight is a wonderful fucking thing. In reality neither you nor the doctors could have predicted what happened.'

'I just hope she can forgive me.'

'I've never known her bear a grudge,' he says, 'She'll come round – wait and see.'

'Easy to say that when you're not the one in the firing line.'

He narrows his eyes at that. 'I offered to talk to her but you insisted on doing it yourself.'

'Well perhaps you should have done; she never gets as angry with you.'

He physically pulls me around to face him. 'Listen – it's not your fault; none of it is. Let's not turn on each other, Lottie.' The front of his hair has fallen into a fringe reminding me of how he looked when we first met. Our breath is smoke – we could be dragons. 'As for what you did or didn't tell Kate beforehand that's not really the point. Okay, you may have played things down a bit but Kate was as nervous as hell about those exams. At the time you did what you thought was best; that's all any of us can do.' He stares into my eyes and waits.

I nod but only to satisfy him.

We continue our walk. Our feet crunch out a rhythm together. The socks over my shoes are heavy with snow. 'P'raps I should phone the hospital,' I say. 'Do I need to make arrangements with a funeral place or something. Oh, God – will they do a postmortem?' It's too late to stop myself from picturing her frail and naked body laid out on a slab about to be cut open.

'I'm pretty sure they won't need to do anything like that,' he says. 'Not when the cause of death is so clear cut. Why don't you let me speak to the hospital and find out what the next steps are?'

I speed up, taking him along with me. 'Okay – that would be good.'

With some force Duncan pushes me into a doorway; I think he's about to kiss me passionately.

There's a silver flash, a jarring thud; looking over his shoulder I see a car's just embedded itself in the lamppost opposite. Steam, or smoke, is pouring out from under the caved-in bonnet. I can just make out the back of the driver's head – the rest of him is engulfed in the airbag.

I'm too stunned to move. Managing to stay on his feet, Duncan runs towards the stricken car.

Off to one side I spot a pedestrian sprawled out in the road. It's the man in the red scarf. He's fallen forward and is face down with both hands outstretched like a penitent.

I make my way over to him and bend down to assess his injures. His head moves a little. Drawing on what I learnt on a first-aid course, I know I should begin by checking that he's breathing. My hand gets as far as his coat. His Chihuahua gives a high-pitched growl and bares its teeth at me – all bulging eyes and sticking-out ears like Yoda gone to the dark side.

The man is moving his arms like someone making snow angels. Moaning and muttering, he attempts to sit up. I scream with pain and shock when razor-like teeth sink into my finger. Startled, the dog lets go its grip to make a yapping retreat.

'Quiet, Archie,' the man says.

'Are you okay?'

'Aye lass, I'm fine. I saw that car skidding towards me and lost me footin' that's all.' Hand under his arm, I help him to his feet. 'Thought it were goin' to run the both us over.'

Across the street, Duncan is still trying to open the driver's door. I slip and slide towards the car – an off-roader with its spare wheel mounted on the back. 'Can't see any other passengers,' Duncan tells me.

Between us we heave and pry the door open. The man inside looks to be unconscious; the inflated airbag makes it seem like he's tucked up under a duvet. I feel under the man's chin and find a definite pulse. It's so cold his breath is visible. 'Shit – where's that blood coming from?' Duncan says.

'I think that's probably mine,' I tell him. 'That dog over there just bit me.'

The man who fell over is now walking towards us dragging the barking culprit.

'Oww! What the fuck?' The driver moves his head. Despite the airbag, there's a livid bruise across the bridge of his nose.

Duncan is on his mobile phoning an ambulance. He relays the necessary information with admirable efficiency and then hangs up. 'They'll get someone here as soon as they can,' he says. 'In the meantime we need to keep him warm.'

He leans in to tell the driver in a loud voice, 'You've had an accident. You're okay but try not to move. Stay as you are. I've phoned for an ambulance – they should be here very soon.' He takes off his coat and drapes it across the driver's shoulders. 'You've suffered a concussion so it's important you remain completely still, just as you are.'

The driver turns his head to peer sideways at us. Then he raises it a bit more and looks around. 'Please, try not to move,' Duncan tells him.

Ignoring instructions, the man slowly sits back in his seat. He looks youngish – around thirty-five or so at a guess. If he didn't shave his head, he'd have a tonsure hairstyle. Staring through the cracked windscreen, he says, 'Shit, that looks bad. Radiator must be knackered for starters.' So he's a Londoner.

Duncan is stamping his feet and rubbing his forearms in an attempt to keep his circulation going. The driver says, 'Here mate, looks to me like you need this more than me.'

'You've had a shock, you need to stay warm and keep still,' I try to tell him.

'No need,' the driver says. 'I'm fine now darlin', honest I am.' Despite Duncan's protestations, the man hands him back his coat. He dismisses our concerns with a wave of his hand. 'Just got a bit of an 'eadache, that's all.' He squeezes past the now floppy airbag and stumbles out of the car.

We step back. Grabbing the wing mirror to stay upright, the man makes his way around to the front of the hissing vehicle. Steam is still pouring out. 'Look at that. An' I just spent five hundred quid on a full fucking service.' Liquid is dripping out of something, forming a golden pool that's spreading out like toffee sauce on the ice.

The driver raises both hands to his head. 'Where the hell's all that bloody oil coming from?' He kicks the wheel and then the lamppost. 'Bollocks,' he says. 'That hurt.'

'You alright?' The man with the scarlet scarf has arrived, his evil yapping dog trailing behind. That scarf – such a colour seems too bright for a man like him. It could belong to his wife or daughter.

Again Duncan tries to intervene. 'You know you really should sit down until they've checked you over. The ambulance will probably be here any minute.'

'Listen, I'm absolutely fine mate,' the driver says, 'though me motor's not looking too clever.'

Scarf-man nods at the driver. 'Engine's been shunted back a fair way. You'll be needing a new rad. Could be all sorts of internals besides.'

We all stare at the hissing car.

Duncan says, 'If you're determined to ignore medical advice, perhaps I should cancel that ambulance. I see no point in wasting their time.'

'Fine by me, mate.' The driver looks around him. 'Suppose there'll be no chance of getting a breakdown truck in this bloody weather. I'll have to leave her here for now, get me mate to pick me up.'

While Duncan makes the call, Scarf-man says, 'Sorry our Archie nipped your hand back there, lass. Never done anything like that before, have ya, eh? Bit shook up I 'spect, what with me falling over and that.'

The dog looks up at me; its liquid eyes are truly black.

'Little lad's never seen snow afore today, have you Arch? Don't you worry – he's had all his shots; still p'raps you ought to put a drop o' peroxide on that – give it a good clean.'

'That your dog then?' the driver asks.

'Aye, if you can call him a dog,' Embarrassed, Scarf-man shakes his head. 'The wife bought it for our eldest last Christmas. Treats it like it were a toy. If I don't take the poor little blighter out, he'd spend all his days indoors. Can't be right, can it?'

Duncan is off the phone. 'As you refuse any further assistance,' he says, 'I think we might as well be on our way.' I'd forgotten how he retreats behind formality when he's really irritated.

'Yeah – thanks again for stopping, mate.' The driver claps Duncan on the back with some vigour. 'Playin' the good Samaritan and all that.'

Despite the pain in my finger, I would liked to have heard more about Scarf-man and his daughter and their snappy little dog.

Taking charge, Duncan steers me away. 'We'd better get that bite of yours cleaned up, Lottie.' He's looking straight ahead, not at me. 'Dogs have millions of bacteria in their mouths. The pharmacists are probably shut so we should go back to the hotel – they'll have a first-aid kit.' Spoken like his university's new Head of Department – a responsible, middle-aged father of two young boys.

Where the sun's hitting it, the ice is melting on the other side of the road and the pavement is less hazardous. Though neither of us says much after that, we manage to set up a rhythm of sorts. Before long I see the hotel's sign up ahead. When the pavement narrows, we let go of each other. I find I can manage okay on my own.

In the hotel lobby, I peel off the socks he lent me. Holding them up, it's clear they'll never be the same again. Without a word, Duncan dumps them in the nearest bin.

We're told the hotel's designated first-aider is still snowed in at home. After a bit of heavy persuasion from Duncan, one of the porters appears with a basic medical kit. I put myself in his hands. Once the wound has been thoroughly cleaned, he cuts off a big enough piece of lint to cover the puncture wounds. Finally, he wraps a gauze bandage around my middle finger and knots it around my thumb.

In a sober mood, we go back up to the suite. On a pad of complimentary headed paper, we draw up a task list. Duncan offers to deal with the official side of things and I'm grateful for it. He sets about this with admirable efficiency. Meanwhile, I draw up a list of the relatives I should contact, most of whom I haven't spoken to in years. It's not a long list – we don't seem to be a very fertile lot.

Though I'd rather not, I feel obliged to start with Kevin, which is a bit awkward given that I called him an arsehole at the end of our last call. It must be around 11 at night for him – a more socially acceptable hour to tell him his mother is dead.

I'm sure he guesses right away why I'm calling again so soon. I get straight to the point. 'I'm really sorry to hear that,' he says like it's my loss and not his.

'It was peaceful at the end,' I tell him hoping he cares. 'She wasn't in pain or anything.'

'That's good.' This is followed by silence, which might mean he's thinking about Mum and everything she must have sacrificed to bring him up, or he doesn't really give a monkey's.

I say, 'Once we've made arrangements for the funeral, I'll let you know all the details. Everyone's welcome, of course.'

'Yeah – thanks Charlie.' He's the only person who ever calls me this; it used to be his pet name for me.

By way of exit, I tell him I have a long list of other calls to get through. 'Yeah, I bet,' he says. 'You take care, sis.' I might have heard a crack in his voice but it could be the poor quality of the line.

It doesn't take long to ring round the other names on my list. Mum must have had friends I know nothing about so, as a catch-all, I compose an announcement for the local paper and phone it in. They deal with it in the same way they might an ad for a used car.

Job done, I strike a pen through my task list, ball it up and aim for the wastepaper basket. Then I rescue it from the floor and drop it in.

Duncan is off the phone. He hands me his copious notes. 'Hopefully, this is all self-explanatory,' he says. It is to a fault-less degree.

I could hug him but instead I put my hand on his arm and say, 'Thank you for doing all that. I really appreciate it.'

His smile could break my heart. 'Can't say it was my pleasure but I'm glad if it helps.'

'I need to get out of here,' I tell him. 'I think I should go back to my hotel and reclaim my belongings before they start thinking I've done a runner.'

My phone pings. I say, 'Kate just sent me a text. She says the trains are running again. She's been told her train should get in around 5:30.'

'Listen, why don't I pick Kate up from the station,' he says. 'I'll drive her over to you.'

I nod. I'm all out of words – so I hug him and leave. I haven't the strength to kiss him goodbye.

Melting Point

Kate arrives cold and wet. Her hug is short and more awkward than it's ever been before. 'Dad dropped me at the door. He wanted to get off right away. I guess it's a long drive.'

When I ask her how she's feeling she says, 'Oh, you know – so-so.'

I do know.

Once she's peeled off her outer layers, she fastens her damp hair away from her face, pinning it through with what looks suspiciously like a chopstick – the takeaway sort.

We're in the lounge of my budget hotel, at a table next to a wide expanse of glass that overlooks the car park. At the other end of the room a group of businesspeople in suits are holding some sort of meeting.

For Kate's sake I've made an effort to look more like my normal self. Straighteners have tamed my hair and I'm wearing mascara and a bit of what Mum used to call foundation. At the bottom of my makeup bag, I found a concealer stick and I hope it's doing an okay job of hiding the circles under my eyes.

Kate notices my bandage. 'What have you done to your hand?'

'Oh that – it's nothing. Someone's nervous little dog nipped me. It looks far worse than it is.'

'Hope you cleaned it well; dogs can carry zoonotic pathogens and –'

'Honestly, it's fine.'

The young waiter who served me earlier comes over eager to take her order. Oblivious to the effect she's having on him, Kate asks about their herbal teas. Blushing a little, he recites the options. 'I'll have a green tea,' she tells him; her 'thanks,' is an afterthought.

Once he's out of earshot she leans forward and says, 'Mum, you might think this is a bit strange, but I want to see Gran's body.' Her face has seldom looked this serious.

'Are you sure? I mean you might find it –'

'I'm quite sure.' Her eyes are solemn and so achingly like Duncan's. 'I know it won't be easy to see her like that, but I've made up my mind.' Bare of any makeup, her skin is flushed from the abrupt temperature change; she looks very like she did at fifteen or sixteen.

Faced with such determination, I'm out of arguments. 'Okay, if that's really what you want.' The thought makes me turn away. Through the glass, I follow a sparrow digging in the margins where the snow has melted. Poor thing must be hungry. Other birds have left their v-shaped footprints everywhere I look.

The waiter comes back with Kate's order and an updated tab. She stirs the tea in front of her more than can be necessary. 'I had a long talk with Freya about it after you phoned,' she says. 'I told her I wanted to see Gran and she thought it was a good idea. It's why I came up here really.'

'I see.'

'Well, you know, of course it's not the only reason. Please don't look at me like that, Mum.' She takes hold of my hand and shakes it. Her fingers are cool to the touch. 'I want, no I *need* to see her before I can accept that it's real – that Gran's gone for good and I'm never going see her again.'

'I understand.' An odd formality has crept into my voice – something I might have learned from Duncan.

There's a dull thud; a minor avalanche of snow has fallen off the roof. It's partly blocking the footpath they've only just cleared. The world outside is melting.

At the other end of the room the businesspeople are now chattering while rearranging chairs in front of a large screen.

I take a very deep breath. 'The funeral director said anyone could visit but I expect we should forewarn them. You know I could go in with you, if you like.'

'*These are the provisional figures for Basingstoke,*' a loud male voice announces.

'I'd rather see her on my own if you don't mind. I wrote a letter to her on the train; put down all the things I want to say to her, not at the funeral but face to face.' She tries a smile. 'I know you don't believe in religion – in the afterlife and all that – but I'm not so sure. Anyway, I want to tell her what she meant to me and I think she might be able to hear me, wherever she is.'

'Maybe she can,' I say. 'I never claimed to have all the answers.'

'*Compare these with Harrogate where, as you can see, sales are down by nineteen percent on this time last year.*'

'I don't mean to upset you, Mum,' she says. 'Seeing Gran is what you might call *closure*.' She does the quotes thing with her fingers. 'You got to say goodbye to her, but I didn't; and I feel I need to.'

'*The Brighton figures paint a very different picture.*'

I blow my nose. 'Okay. I'll give the funeral home a ring this afternoon.'

'Thanks for understanding,' she says.

People are clapping. '*Great teamwork, Sally and Raheem.*' They all stand up and shake hands like a non-conformist congregation. '*Obviously, we'll need time to digest your full report before this afternoon's break-out sessions.*' Once they've run out of hands to shake, they peel off in twos and threes.

'Please don't look like that,' Kate says.

'I'm really sorry, Kate. When she went into hospital I didn't think it was that serious. I really didn't expect – '

'I know; I know.' She grabs my arm. 'Listen, I was angry and upset when I said those things to you – I didn't mean them. Gran was pretty old. At Christmas I noticed how frail she was looking. And she'd lost all that weight and that.'

I say, 'I didn't say goodbye to her properly – like I wanted to.'

'But you still can.' She pulls the napkin from underneath the biscuits neither of us have touched. 'Don't go all guilt ridden on me, Mum. Dad told me he looked in on Gran at the hospital and they explained there'd been unexpected problems during her op.'

Though I'm grateful for his intervention, I wonder what else Duncan has told her; like co-conspirators we need to get our stories straight.

'Quite a coincidence wasn't it?'

'Sorry, I missed that bit. What was a coincidence?'

'Dad being up here for a conference at the same time.'

Trying to sound off-hand I say, 'I suppose he must go to lots of those things – now he's Head of Department.'

'Still, it makes you think, you know, about fate and all that stuff.'

'Yes, I suppose it does.'

The businesspeople file out past our table to the exit and I watch them encounter the snowfall like cats not wanting to get their feet wet.

Kate reaches over to rub my shoulder. 'Listen, you're not a bloody clairvoyant, Mum. You couldn't have known what would happen.'

'Still, I'm sorry.'

'What for this time? You're allowed to be upset – she was your mother after all.'

'I don't seem to be making very good decisions at the moment,' I tell her. 'Not only about Gran but about other things in my life.'

She holds her mouth in the way she does when she's uncertain. 'Don't know if I should say this, if you want to hear it even, but I think you made the right decision when you split up with Michael. Don't get me wrong, I mean he's fundamentally a decent man and all that; it's just the two of you are very different.'

This at least makes me smile. 'Don't worry,' I tell her. 'That is one decision I definitely don't regret.'

'Good,' she says. She opens up the red plastic menu. 'Did

I tell you I saw him – Michael that is – on the news the other day?'

'Wait, you actually watch the news now?'

She grins. 'To be honest, I was waiting for something else to come on.'

'I saw him too,' I tell her, 'though I could hardly watch. There were bullets flying around his head, but I have to say, he looked like he was in his element.'

'He loves all that,' she says. 'You know there's this boy at uni who was always doing crazy – I mean stupidly dangerous things. His parents took him off to psych and she told him how the brains of people who are high sensation seekers release way more dopamine when they're doing dangerous stuff. It's actually a recognised addiction.'

'Maybe that's the answer,' I say.

'Oh, and talking of uni stuff, my tutor emailed me. He says I don't need to sit the last exam – they're going to base my mark on coursework, which is good news.' She sips her tea. 'Overall, I think the rest of the exams went okay – quite well, in fact. Better than the last lot, that's for sure.'

'That's great. I'm so proud of you.'

'Don't overdo it, Mum, I haven't had the marks back yet.' Kate pulls a face. 'The food here is really bad. Everything comes with chips. No salads. D'you think there's a sushi place around here?'

'Are you sure you're a student?' I drain my tea. 'I mean sushi – since when did you get so sophisticated?'

'Since I noticed how much better my skin looks if I don't eat crap.'

A lot of the shops and cafés are still shut. It's far too wet and cold to trail around looking for a Japanese restaurant and so, attracted by the homely smells, we settle on an organic café. My shoes don't grip so well without Duncan's socks.

Candles burn on each table despite it being midday. The daily specials have been chalked on a dusty blackboard on the wall behind the pine counter. After a quick glance, I order their quiche-of-the-day with the house salad. Kate takes some time procrastinating before she opts for what promises to be a Thai-style noodle dish.

It's just after noon and we are the only diners apart from a loved-up couple near the door and a man with a grey and straggly ponytail slurping his soup.

We choose a table well away from them though we talk about nothing of consequence – a tacit understanding not to revisit our previous conversation.

The place begins to fill up; each time the door opens an icy blast steals in. The food is a welcome distraction – hearty portions piled up on handmade pottery plates. Speaking only for myself, the food tastes as good as it looks. Kate says hers is fine though she toys with it. She pushes the rest aside after eating half. On a different occasion I might have offered to finish it off.

She checks her phone while I go to pay the bill. As we're leaving Kate says, 'I just saw something Simone posted on Instagram.' When I look blank, she says, 'You do know what Instagram is, right?'

'Damned cheek.' I dig her in the ribs. 'Do I know this Simone?'

We skirt round a particularly large puddle.

'You must remember her – she was in my year at school? We did maths together?' I recall a group of girls dressed identically in hitched-up navy skirts. 'Simone came round ours quite a few times. She's tall, skinny. Pretty but with a biggish nose. Wore loads of makeup, even for school.'

'Oh her.' It's easier to pretend.

'Anyway, she's got back with her loser boyfriend. Talk about toxic relationships. She just posted this picture of them with their arms round each other like nothing's happened. I mean I know I haven't had many relationships and all that but I'd never take someone back after they'd cheated on me.'

I do my best to shrug this away. 'She must still like him.'

'Yeah, maybe. Though, knowing her, I'd say she's probably just desperate not to be the one who got dumped. I wouldn't be surprised if she waits a bit and then dumps him in the middle of a party – when she's got a suitable audience.'

Though there's very little traffic, we wait for the green man. I'm still trying to place this girl. 'Really? She'd do something like that just to save face?'

'You don't know Simone. For her it's all about what other people think. She hasn't got over the humiliation of being the one who was cheated on.'

I look at her lovely face. 'You know, Kate,' I say, 'it's possible you're more grown-up now than I've ever been.'

We agree to separate. I hand Kate my keycard and she heads back to the hotel to warm up. I set off alone to find a cash machine. The pavements are still slippery in places – potential accidents await a momentary lack of attention.

It doesn't take long to find a hole in the wall. While I'm standing there, a passing car ploughs straight through a puddle of slushy water sending an icy spray over my feet and up the back of my trousers. Like the mature woman I am, I shout obscenities after the driver.

I buy a pack of plasters to replace my now grubby bandage.

Opposite the pharmacy there's a shoe shop, which is open. I search along lines of boots for a pair with sensible heels and a decent tread. I keep turning them upside-down but can't find any that would be suitable for the conditions outside. Every shoe in the men's section fits the bill perfectly but they're all too big. Do shoe designers expect women to be carried shoulder high by some hunk through icy streets?

I have a bit of a rant about this to the stoically indifferent shop assistant. Before I leave, I check my mobile for messages and see I've missed a call from Duncan. It may be the coward's way out but I don't have the bandwidth to speak to him right now.

I pick my way back to the hotel. The lobby is full of Japanese people looking bewildered. I skirt around them. Though the lift is crowded, it smells of spring blossoms – a pumped-in chemical freshener to mask any human scent.

Music greets me as the lift doors part. I follow it down the corridor and knock on the door of my room. It opens and the music is at maximum volume. 'Hi, Mum,' she says, big smile. Her head is wrapped in a towel and she's changed into a baggy t-shirt and sweat pants. When she flicks a remote, the music subsides but only fractionally.

Behind her, the room has lost its anonymity; it's been

customised into a chaotic mess. 'Dad phoned while you were out.' Her voice is breezy, matter-of-fact. 'He wants you to give him a ring when you have a moment.'

She unwraps the wet towel and throws it onto the dry bedspread. Running her fingers through her damp hair she says, 'For some reason he already knew the name of the funeral home, so anyway I rang them myself and they were really nice. I've arranged to see Gran tomorrow morning at 10:30.'

I pick up the towel, find my hairbrush and hand it to her. 'If you're planning to go to Gran's house,' she says, 'I'd like to come too. We could go through her things together.'

Recalling Mum's words, I pull a face though Kate's too busy brushing her hair to notice. She says, 'There must be some old photos of her we could get copied for the funeral – the leaflet thingy they give you as you go in.'

A flick of the head and her long hair flies up and lands behind her back like a circus trick. 'They did that at Aunty Jean's funeral. It's a way of reminding you they weren't always old and sick.'

'Who's Aunty Jean?'

'On Dad's side,' she says. 'His mum's sister? Died of breast cancer a couple of years back.'

I vaguely recall meeting her at our wedding – smiley woman, a shorter and a bit rounder version of his mum. Someone Duncan was apparently fond of though I only saw her once more after that.

I can't face ringing Duncan – not after all that's happened. Sitting down, I unwrap the soiled bandage on my hand and examine my finger. It seems to be healing well – no sign of infection. It's possible it will leave a line of tiny scars. I'm sure no one will notice except me.

Keepsakes

Kate and I are alone in the house – Mum's house. We still have our coats on because it's cold; the heating is set to only come on to keep the temperature above freezing. I crank the old-fashioned thermostat up several more notches and hear the boiler kick in. A futile gesture – it would take an age to warm this place up.

Kate rushes upstairs to the bathroom while I survey the things Mum prized; it makes me sad to see them abandoned and unloved. She would be upset that her furniture is now covered in a fine layer of dust. Most of the big items will be auctioned so I should give them one final polish; they deserve to be presented in the best possible light. I doubt the valuer they send round will get excited about any of it, but it's good to think of new owners cherishing the post-war table we used to sit at or the Victorian prints she was so fond of. I plan to keep the worn leather armchair that once belonged to the grandfather I never met. I hope Kate will choose one or two keepsakes.

She hasn't reappeared so I go upstairs to see what she's up

to. I find her in Mum's bedroom sitting on the bed. Behind her, Mum's beloved embroidered box is lying empty; gaping at me like an open mouth. The things I assume must have been inside it have been arranged in separate piles on the bedspread.

'There's some great old photos here,' Kate says. 'Definitely one or two we could use at the funeral. And there's a bunch of letters from Australia.' She holds up a pile of faded blue airmails bound by an elastic band.

'Take a look at this, Mum.' She hands me a loose pile of things. 'She cut out loads of your book reviews and things and, look, the notifications letter with your exam results.' I examine each one – can hardly believe that Mum had spent time assembling this little archive of my achievements.

'All the same, Kate, I really don't think you should have opened it. This is Mum's private stuff – we have to put it all back right now.'

'Calm down. I was just curious to see what was in it, that's all.'

I pick up the empty box and check it for damage. 'I've wanted to know that most of my life.'

Kate says, 'I remember Gran showing me this box when I was staying with her one time. She wouldn't let me open it though. They call that stitch needlepoint, apparently. Gran's mum – my great-grandma – embroidered that centre panel with the pansies. Gran told me the smaller ones are called violas like the instruments. She said people used to call violas Johnny-jump-ups because they spread so easily and you can eat them.'

'And you remember all that?'

She shrugs. 'I'm young, young people's brains retain information better.'

'Do they? I must have forgotten.'

'Ha ha.'

'So did she tell you anything else about it?'

'She said she stitched that border herself when she was just a girl. Apparently, her mother had been impressed by a hanky she'd embroidered and so she said she trusted her not to spoil it.'

'Really? I never knew all that.' I turn the box around in my hands and notice a few places where the silk threads are faded. 'Did she tell you who made the box itself – the wooden part?'

Kate shakes her head. 'If she did, I don't remember.'

'That young brain of yours isn't infallible then.'

She smiles. 'Unfortunately not.'

I look at the stitching and imagine Carol's young fingers threading the needle through and back over and over, time after time, making sure every stitch was perfectly the same as the next one. A real labour of love. 'She certainly did a great job but the flowers in the centre are even more impressive.'

'Must have taken them hours and hours between them,' Kate says.

'Their idea of recreation, I suppose. Of course they didn't have a telly when Mum was little in the forties. They might have had a radio in the twenties when my grandma Betty was a child – if they could afford one.'

When I sniff, the inside of the box is musty – the smells of forgotten secrets. I say, 'We should put this all back. I mean it. Mum would be so angry at the two of us for going through her private things.'

'No need to make a drama out of it,' Kate says. 'You make it sound like that box in Raiders of the Lost Ark.'

The two of us watched that film together. 'I remember you kept grabbing my arm in the scary bits,' I tell her.

'I was terrified in that bit when they opened the ark and it looked empty at first; then this gigantic demon materialised and killed everyone.'

'But in the end Harrison Ford and the girl survive because they shut their eyes and don't look.'

She frowns. 'Are you suggesting there's a lesson in that?'

I put the empty box down on the bedside table. 'They said something at the very end about the ark going to a safe place to be studied?' My finger traces the outline of the purple flowers on the lid – their tiny yellow centres. 'You have to wonder how they could study it with their eyes shut.'

Kate laughs. 'Robots? Remote cameras?' She looks at me, then the box, then me again. 'Now I've opened it, perhaps I've exorcised its demons.'

'I've actually been wondering if we should bury it with her.'

'Seems like a waste of all the work they put into it.'

'You're right, it does. And I suppose I might regret it later – like Dante Rossetti regretted burying his poems in poor Lizzie Siddal's coffin.'

'Wasn't he driven by guilt?'

'He was,' I say. 'But then, aren't we all?'

Laid to Rest

At least the rain has held off – for the moment anyway. The setting for this church and its graveyard must have been appropriately dramatic when it was built four hundred years ago. Swept by high winds that bent the tall trees surrounding it, on fine days your eye would have been able to run between the gaps in their trunks to the open ground and on to the purple topped moor beyond. Since then the ancient trees have been pollarded – their limbs mercilessly cut down to a more manageable size; they look emasculated. You could almost be in a suburban park. Despite its spire, the grey-faced church seems to squat in the centre of the remaining open space; shrunk in on itself; hemmed in all around by the massed ranks of housing and light industrial units.

None of it is how I imagined it would be.

Mum told me several times that she wanted to be buried. A straightforward request – a two metre or so stretch of earth on the outskirts of your hometown. Not much to ask for, one would have thought. Over the phone, the vicar had disabused me of such an assumption. He'd explained that they'd more or less run out of new plots. I noticed he didn't say who had dibs on the last few. He talked me through the limited number of options left. In the end, it was my decision to bury Mum with Dad; to make them closer in death than they had been in life. What choice did I have? It was either that, or a cremation plot near the outer ring road.

It's not going to be a dignified, arm's length, side-by-side arrangement. Instead they've opened Dad's grave to more or less dump Mum on top. 'There won't be much left in there anyway,' the young Reverend Lewis had assured me, seeming to forget he was referring to my father's earthly remains. He'd called round to discuss the matter when I was sorting out her house. 'I'm afraid nothing lasts long in that soil,' he said, his dark eyes crinkling with a practiced smile.

I think, though the headstones are now too worn to be faithfully deciphered, that she'll be resting quite near to the bones of her own mum and dad – or at least the remnants of their bones.

I've arrived early because I'm as nervous as a hostess before the start of a milestone party. Kate isn't even here yet – she's getting a lift from Duncan. They are the only two people I really care about.

Looking around, it's clear from all the stacked-up stone slabs that, on the quiet, there's a recycling process going on even here. The vicar let slip that any unvisited grave is likely, in time, to get re-used for someone else. Obscurity is lying in wait and ready to snatch back whatever might have otherwise remained to tell a tale to future generations. It's not like the dead can object or speak up for themselves.

Mum couldn't have anticipated that the frozen ground would keep us all waiting until her grave could be dug. I didn't expect the delay either; such things seem almost farcical to the modern mind.

It's a relief when cars begin to arrive, when sombrely dressed people begin to walk through the old lychgate in twos and threes. I needn't have worried; it looks like it's going to be quite a decent turnout.

My phone pings with another text from Kate – they've now cleared the hold-up though they're still likely to be a few minutes late. I would rather not make small talk with the congregation, so I retreat into the church.

The vicar promised they'd put the heating on but still the place makes me shiver, but then churches were never meant to make you feel comfortable. There are a few thin tapestry cushions but, leaving them for others more in need, I sit down on the hard, unforgiving pew. Copies of the booklet Kate put together have been placed on the pews. A smiling Carol at twenty-eight reminds me she was once a dark-haired, good-looking young woman. On the inside cover there's a grainy family shot of her at the seaside with my brother and me. Dad must have taken it. It looks chilly but our smiles are warm. On the back cover Mum is lifting a giggling baby Katie up in the air. They have eyes only for each other.

Behind me I hear the sounds of people shuffling in; of throats being cleared and whispered greetings. I recognise some of them and we exchange the sort of quick smile people give when they're trying to be respectful of the occasion.

I stare at young Carol, at the dates of her birth and death seventy-eight years apart.

'Hi, Mum.' Kate startles me. She sits down beside me and we give each other an awkward sideways hug. 'Sorry we're so late,' she whispers. 'The queues were ridiculous.'

Duncan sits down beside her. He's looking straight ahead. 'You're here now,' I tell her. 'That's all that matters.'

I don't think I would have recognised my brother if he hadn't made his way up to the front pew. A formidable figure, he stands in the aisle waiting to claim his rightful place while everyone shuffles along to accommodate him. He seems shorter than I'd remembered. If we passed in the street I wouldn't have known him but then I never did – not really.

As the heavy chords of the first hymn ring out, the colours in the stained glass are simultaneously lit up from behind for one glorious moment. When the sun goes in, the glass dulls again. How easy it would be to see this as a divine sign.

The prelude over, I look behind and see the people holding Kate's leaflet high and opening and closing their mouths. We all struggle to keep pace with the organist. I have no idea who most of them are. From their age, I would guess some are former workmates. I vaguely recognise a few neighbours past and present.

The stonework is doing all it can to concentrate the bitter cold. Our depleted family is standing up together, even if we're not exactly shoulder-to-shoulder. Kate is now leaning sideways into Duncan. The arm he has around her brushes my shoulder. Alongside him I glimpse the blonde hair of Sarah, his wife. Thank goodness I didn't encounter the two of them outside; I'm not ready to look her in the face. Someone's heavy perfume is permeating the air; I turn my head and recognise the imposing figure of Mum's only remaining sister – my Aunty Margaret. Seated just behind her are her children – my cousins Toby and Sally, plus Sally's husband Geoff. For some reason they'd written to say they were coming otherwise I would struggle to recognise any of them.

Leaning forward, I sneak another look at Kevin. His hair is totally white now; against his deep tan it looks like he's become his own negative. His body has grown sturdy – some might say fat – and there's a new stoop to his shoulders. He's chosen to sit next to the aisle in what might be considered the chief mourner's position and now he's singing in a deep, loud voice that seems to carry further than anyone else's. Kevin flew in only yesterday, apparently unaccompanied. I hope he's here because deep inside he's discovered a lingering affection for the widowed young mother who struggled to raise him. To my certain knowledge, he's already spoken to the solicitor to check that the legalities are being dealt with in the correct manner.

Kate has chosen to read "Remember" the Christina Rossetti poem. I had to suppress the urge to tell her she doesn't have to do it because I know she does.

We sit down. Kate remains standing. She's visibly shaking. Thank goodness it's a short poem. I can hardly bear to watch her make her way to the front of the church all on her own. The vicar comes forward, guides her on with an outstretched hand to the lectern.

Kate knows the words by heart but her delivery is fresh and moving. I'm so proud of her and how she manages to get through the whole thing without breaking down.

Standing between us, she sings the next hymn without faltering. The congregation sits down and now it's my turn.

I've written a short eulogy and I'm gripping the piece of paper it's written on for dear life. As convention dictates, I'm starting with a bit about her childhood – the deprivations the family lived through before and after the war. It wouldn't be right not to mention her first dead husband, Kevin's father. I haven't said that much about her meeting my dad, other than the obvious. Thanks to the phonebook I found at the house, I'd spoken to two of her old colleagues and managed to piece together a few things about Mum's life when she was not being my mother. I've kept it short – only a couple of paragraphs sum up her long career in what was then called *auxiliary nursing*. No one mentioned any funny anecdotes I could retell to lighten the mood.

Rule number one, it said on the undertaker's website, is to keep your eulogy short. Last night, when I read through what I'd written, I realised it wasn't nearly enough. How could it be? Now, I'm more worried that I won't be able to get past the first paragraph.

I have to squeeze past Duncan, Sarah and lastly Kevin – who has the good sense to step aside. It seems a long walk down the echoing aisle. I spread the paper out on the lectern in front of me and try to pretend this is just another book reading. I know I should, but I can't look at my audience, at the congregation; any sympathetic expression might set me off.

I tell the high arches: 'Some of you might have known my mother when she was Carol Webb, or possibly Carol Meakins.' I glance at my brother – it's an acknowledgement of the surname they once shared. 'To others she was Carol Preece, or just Carol, or Mum, or Gran.'

Staring at the raised font at the back, I begin to ad lib. 'When I say we *knew* her, what does that really mean? We might have recognised her voice, her face in its various incarnations as she aged; but how much did any of us understand about the person that was Carol?'

My gaze sinks to the tops of heads. 'I know, when I was growing up, there might have been days, weeks even, when I hardly noticed her, not really. Though I carried on benefiting from all the things she did for me, for my brother and my dad.'

I look directly at Kevin, at his perma-tanned features and thinning hair. Perhaps my expression betrays me, reveals the accusations I might make but stop short of. In any case he's already turned away, might not even be listening.

'The truth is, I was too preoccupied. I wasn't what you might describe these days as *there* for her. Not when she needed it. She must have been distraught when my brother Kevin left to build his own life thousands of miles away in Australia. I was too wrapped up in my own grief, I'm ashamed to admit it, when my dad died so suddenly.'

I'm not expressing myself the way I would have liked. There's a danger this is becoming rather maudlin. I take a breath, glance down the aisle to where a peal of coughs is ringing out. When they finally subside, I too feel calmer. My hands smooth the piece of paper out, but I can't see the words I've written anymore.

'I know when this day is over, I will have done all the practical things required of me as a daughter. But will I visit the grave outside?' I look towards Reverend Lewis. 'A few times maybe; after that, far less often.'

My mind is struggling to form the words I need. 'But, whether I choose it or not, Mum is here.' My closed fist beats my breast. 'In this body that she gave birth to and nourished; in all the things she taught me throughout her life; and most of all in my memory of her unwavering love and pride in me. These are the things that will endure: a legacy that I can only strive, in turn, to pass on.'

The tears I held back begin to flow. I'm aware of soaring silence as I walk back to the front pew. It's hard to know whether I'm shivering or shaking as I wait for Kevin to make room for me to pass by. He stands up – leans in to whispers, 'Well done, Charlie.'

Once we're back outside it seems warmer though the wind that stings our faces carries tiny particles of snow. The threatened bad weather has held off – but for how long?

At the graveside we gather around. I look down at the flowers Kate and I chose resting so precariously on the top of Mum's coffin; their petals tremble as they're lowered into the grave. Dad's remains are beneath her; the ring that bound them together is still there on her finger.

Directed by Reverend Lewis, we take turns to throw handfuls of soil onto the coffin lid; as each one hits the target it makes a blunt, callous sound. After that the vicar shakes a few hands, repeats his condolences, and then walks away. I'm left staring into the hole.

Kate squeezes my arm and I close my hand around hers.

She's shivering. I notice people have started to leave – not surprising given how bitterly cold it is.

I turn Kate around and guide her away from the graveside. Duncan and his wife block our retreat. Sarah crosses in front of him to give me a couple of air kisses at arm's length. She declares herself, 'Sorry for your loss.' The phrase suggests a certain carelessness on my part. Kate is now sobbing into Duncan's chest and he hugs her while kissing the top of her head. I know he'll look after her.

One old woman breaks away from a group of women around the same age and comes over to speak to me. Her gloved hand touches my arm. 'Hello, Lottie,' she says. 'Don't s'pose you remember me. I thought I'd better make myself known. I'm Sadie Robinson – I worked with your mam years ago.' The glimmer in her eyes suggests liveliness behind the heavy disguise of old age.

I'm taken aback when she says, 'You always did favour your father.'

'I don't think that's true. I mean I certainly didn't intend to. I loved them both in different ways, it's just that–'

The gloved hand squeezes my arm. 'Only that you've got his eyes, dear. Your colouring is different – you're not as dark as yer mam was, that's for sure.'

'Oh I see. Yes of course.'

'It gave me quite a shock when I saw the announcement in the paper. Good job I did else I wouldn't have known she'd passed away.'

Since when did we stop using the word died? 'Gave me quite a turn I don't mind telling you. Aye, it were a shame we lost touch, yer mam and me.' She looks sad for a moment then shrugs. 'I suppose I moved away and – what with this and that...'

'Won't you come back to the house – it's not far. We're having a bit of a get together for her family and friends.'

Sadie lets go of my arm. 'Sorry, dear. Love to stop an' have a natter but my son-in-law's picking me up.' She looks over her shoulder as if he might be standing there. 'Anyroad, I just wanted to say how fond I was of yer mam and how sorry I am she's no longer with us.'

My cousin Toby looms over her shoulder. 'It's been a bloody long time, Lottie,' he says muscling in. 'Must be fifteen years at least. Heard you was living in London and writing books for a living.' He shakes his head. ''Fraid I haven't had time to read any of 'em but then I'm more of a history man meself.'

Behind him, Sadie has already reached the lychgate. She waves at a man standing by a blue car and he waves back.

Turning to Toby, I force myself to ask, 'So what are you up to these days?'

'This an' that.' Like he's sparring, his head ducks one way and then the other. When I check again, Sadie has already been whisked away.

Gathering

In the back of the big black limousine we hold hands. Kate is still trembling so I put my arm around her and ask if she's okay. Despite her tears she nods. I rub up and down her arm hoping it will make a difference. She says, 'I keep reminding myself how peaceful Gran looked – more like she'd fallen asleep watching telly.' I hand her a tissue and she blows her nose. 'Stupid I know but I kept expecting her to wake up.'

It's as much as I can do to hold it together, but I must if I'm going to get through the rest of the day.

Rather than an anonymous hotel, we decided to hold the funeral tea at Mum's house. Can't remember whose idea it was but it seemed like the right one at the time. Now I'm not so sure.

We're the first inside. Earlier, I'd cranked up the heating and, though it may be on its last legs, the boiler hasn't let me down. If she were here, Mum would shake her head and turn down the dial on the thermostat. She always complained about the degree of warmth in my house – unhealthy was the word she liked to use.

Kate heads for the upstairs toilet. I hang up my coat where I've always hung it and, ignoring the buffet the caterers have laid on, search out the alcohol.

There aren't that many of us but Mum's small front room is soon packed out. It's so strange to think of this gathering of the clans taking place in her honour and her not being here to enjoy it.

A local firm of estate agents is planning to erect a For Sale sign in the garden tomorrow morning; a signal for total strangers to begin to pry into every corner, open all her cupboard doors.

I pour myself a double whisky and down it as swiftly as seems decent. It warms my throat then hits my empty stomach like acid. I seem to be acquiring a taste for Scotch. Armed with a generous refill, I get ready to play my part and mingle.

As befits the new head of the family, Aunty Margaret is already ensconced in an armchair and accepting the refreshments brought to her by her children. Mum's phrase *waited on hand and foot* comes to mind. Seeing me, she repeats her commiserations and then begins to catalogue her own recent ailments as if the two of them had been in some sort of gruesome competition and Mum had unsportingly romped home on the inside. Tackling a mini Scotch egg, she tells me, 'Course my legs aren't what they were.' Given the size of her, this is undeniable. I find myself becoming mesmerised by the way she's eating. Due to the impediment of what are clearly false teeth, she's developed a sort of sucking technique that puts me in mind of a ladybird beetle hoovering up greenfly. Most impressively, she can eat and continue a monologue almost uninterrupted. I'm simply required to nod or make sympa-thetic noises whenever she pauses to swallow the next item from the piled up plate she's working her way through.

Ten long minutes later, I spot Kate heading in our direction. I step into her path, lean in and say, 'I'm taking one for the team here.' In order to make myself clear, I execute a theatrical wink. 'Your great aunt is a martyr to her arthritis,' I whisper. 'Better save yourself while you can.'

After a 'Hi, Aunty – nice to see you again,' Kate wisely joins her dad and Sarah. Both have their backs to me but I hear the latter declare, 'Black really does suit you, honey. You should wear it more often.' Sarah puts her arm around Kate's waist in a motherly gesture, which I know I have no right to resent, though I do.

Sarah barely knew Mum and yet the woman is dressed head-to-toe in black, even down to the small pillbox hat with a tiny veil perched atop her blonde hair. You might take her for one of the chief mourners instead of my ex-husband's plus one. She's taken off her coat but left the hat in place. I picture her ordering it from some website specialising in funeral chic.

I can't remember the last time I saw Duncan in a suit. This one's dark blue and not especially funereal. He's wearing a white shirt; only his tie is black. Perhaps he can sense that I'm looking at him because he turns and gives me a wide smile that would melt my heart if I were to let it.

Following his gaze, Sarah sees me and forces an altogether tighter smile to her lips. Her face drops sharply as she turns away. Does she suspect something has gone on behind her back? Thanks to the whisky, my conscience has been temporarily knocked out. Draining the rest of my glass, I watch her offer Duncan a salmon blini – she actually puts it in his mouth. The man's almost fifty-years-old, surely he can feed himself.

Of course, I'm not being the least bit fair or balanced but today I don't fucking care. I've just buried my mother, after all.

When my cousin Toby arrives, Margaret's attention turns to the food on his plate and the possibility she might have missed out on something he has. 'Speak to you later,' I tell them with no intention of doing so if I can help it.

I'm refilling my glass when my other cousin, Sally, links her arm with mine and draws me aside to ask me how I'm bearing up. It's just possible she's steering me away from the booze. 'Been better,' I tell her.

Leaning in she says, 'You poor thing,' in a tone you might use if a child had fallen over. 'Must have been quite a shock your mum going like that.' She snaps her fingers. 'We none of us expected it.'

Sally's husband Geoff appears. He plants a wet kiss on my cheek giving me the opportunity to disentangle myself from his wife's grip. After years in London, I automatically offer Geoff the other cheek but he doesn't respond. Instead, he nods towards his mother-in-law. 'Listening to her majesty the Princess Margaret over there you'd think she didn't have long for this world. My guess is she'll outlive us all. Only thing likely to dispatch her is a stake through the ruddy heart.'

'Stop it, Geoff.' His wife digs an elbow in his side. 'Shush, for heaven's sake she might hear you.'

He snorts. 'The old bat claims to be hard of hearing but I think she's switched to echo location.'

Sally rolls her eyes – a what's-he-like gesture that seems like it's much practiced. 'Aunty Carol was such a special lady,' she says. 'Pity we didn't get to see her very often. Course our grandkids keep us busy these days. Did you know our Elaine had twin boys last June? She works part-time as a dentist's receptionist so we look after Eddie and Freddie Tuesday to Thursday during the week, don't we Geoff?'

'Aye, we do,' he says without enthusiasm.

'Bet you can't wait till you're a granny,' Sally says.

I take a sip of my whisky. 'Kate's only just had her twentieth birthday,' I tell her. 'She's still got two more years at uni.'

She looks over at Kate and says, 'Pretty girl.'

'Aye she is that.' Geoff agrees with worrying enthusiasm.

Sally says, 'Don't s'pose it'll be long before some young man snaps her up.' This time I'm the one who get a dig in the ribs. She nods at me like we're both in on a secret.

Mrs Harbottle is heading for the door. 'Excuse me but I really ought to have a word with Mum's neighbour before she leaves,' I tell them. 'Nice to see you both again.' And with that I'm most definitely off.

In my peripheral vision, I'd vaguely noticed Kevin eying up the picture on the wall. He's wearing a serious expression when he intercepts me. Mrs Harbottle has already made her exit. 'I've been meaning to talk to you about Mum's will,' Kevin says. No preamble, no how are you bearing up – this is a money matter, after all.

I know he's been giving Mum's solicitors a hard time despite the fact that they drew up a very detailed and comprehensive will for her in 2008. She made the two of us joint beneficiaries as I would have expected. The only exception is a clause allowing Kate and myself to choose any furniture or household items we might wish to keep before the rest of her effects are sold off.

He gets close enough for me to smell onion on his breath. 'Thing is, I'm not sure Mum would have had any idea what some of this stuff might be worth these days.'

I nearly laugh in his face. It's not like the place is stuffed full of valuable antiques. 'Funny you should say that,' I say, 'she did have quite an eye for art.' I survey the walls before asking, 'Do you know anything about art, Kevin?'

'Not a lot.' He shrugs, seems to be pleased with his ignorance.

'Well, as you can see, over the years Mum amassed quite a collection. She had a particular thing for works by the Pre-Raphaelite Brotherhood.'

'You've lost me there.'

'They were a famous, some might say infamous group of Victorian artists – painters, poets and so on. Their work is highly sought after these days.' I raise my glass to her taste. 'See that one over there by the door with the plain-faced, some might say ugly woman and her miserable looking child?'

'Yeah.' He snorts. 'Certainly not what you'd call a looker, is she?'

'Quite. You probably wouldn't guess it was painted by one of the lesser known members of the group – James Collinson.'

'No kidding.'

'Now see the one right next to it with the three women gathered around a pyramid of dead leaves? That one's an actual Millais.'

The colour drains from his face. I guess he's heard the name before. 'No shit!' Eyes on steroids, he spins round and is obviously calculating the number of paintings in this room alone.

I allow myself a couple of minutes while he loosens his collar and readies himself for the next round of combat. 'Unfortunately,' I say, 'they're all prints. Reproduced in the thousands and…'

I pause to look directly into his face, 'More or less worthless, I'm sad to say.' On that note I walk away.

I'm coming back from the loo when Duncan intercepts me at the bottom of the stairs. He literally blocks my path with his feet planted firmly apart. 'You won't take my calls,' he says. 'You won't answer my texts and now you're actively avoiding me like I've done something wrong.'

My eyes dart past him into the hallway to check we're alone – that no one is about to overhear this. Lowering my voice to a whisper I say, 'What do you expect – am I supposed to stand around making polite conversation with you in front of your wife?' I hold up my hands. 'I'm sorry, Duncan but I simply can't do it.'

He checks behind then leans forward to say, 'Kate's noticed how oddly you're behaving towards me – she just asked me if we'd had a row.'

'Shit.'

'Exactly. Listen, we really need to talk.'

I shake my head and say, 'I can't do this right now.'

'Then when? Lottie there are things – I mean, you and I need to have a civilised, grown up conversation.'

'Don't talk to me like I'm an adolescent – like I'm one of your fucking students.'

The sitting room door opens. I recognise Mr Jones – the man who lives across the road. Duncan turns his back. Sensing he's stumbled into something, the poor man looks embarrassed. His eyes dart from me to Duncan and back. 'Hope I'm not interrupting,' he says. 'Your daughter said the bathroom was upstairs.'

'Yes, of course.' I move out of the way of his considerable belly.

We watch his breathless progress up the stairs. When he finally closes the bathroom door Duncan says, 'This may not be the ideal time, but–'

'No,' I tell him. 'This is not the ideal time; I think we can agree on that at least.'

To make my point I walk away. Wondering if this day could possibly get any worse, I take the coward's way out and head for more alcohol.

One Last Time

The funeral and all it entailed has kept me occupied – preoccupied. Now it's over, it ushers in a strange hiatus. There are still things to be sorted out but none of it requires my urgent attention. It's time I went home; faced my own particular music.

I arrive just as early dusk is giving way to nightfall. The Fiat struggles with the last miles or so; it's a relief when I finally pull into the building's underground garage. Even though it's a small car, it's not easy to back it into my dedicated parking spot between the fire escape door and a concrete pillar. I leave my humble car to its well-earned rest amongst the Range Rovers and Mercedes.

Walking into my flat alone my footsteps seem louder than before. Ambient light from outside is casting shadows that make the familiar unfamiliar. I've always found the overhead lights too harsh – they really mean business. Instead I put on a couple of lamps. Though I haven't been away for that long, it feels strange to be back.

From across the room the view attracts me like it always

does. The cold air hits me as soon as I open the balcony doors. Sounds of the city rise up to greet me in the usual cacophony, the endless soundtrack to other people's busy lives.

I go back inside, turn off the lamps and then go back out to stand in the city's fugitive light. Thanks to concrete's ability to store heat, the temperature is a little warmer than it was up north – already a world away. So many lighted windows; every office building is twinkling like Christmas – a celebration of wealth with a profligate disregard for the cost.

I trace the path of the river as it snakes between those high lit-up towers. Across each bridge more modest lights hang in skeins stretching from one support to the next like necklaces. I'm not a Londoner by birth but this sprawling, beautiful and ugly city is where I've always felt most at home.

After what's happened, how can I pick up the threads of my old life?

I think about Michael – the way he struggled to come down from such heightened emotions every time he returned. How insignificant my everyday preoccupations and concerns must have seemed to him.

The cold soon sends me back inside. After shutting the balcony doors and pulling the sheer curtains across, the room seems a lot cozier. I walk over to my desk and turn the lamp on and it illuminates the manuscript of my unfinished novel.

It's still sitting where I put it after snatching it from Duncan's hands. I should never have printed the damned thing out, wasted all that paper on something I'm never going to finish. If I'm to find a way forward, the first thing I need to do is jettison this particular millstone.

Duncan was right about that; he was right about a lot of things.

Setting fire to all that paper would only set off the fire alarms. Besides it's not very green. I haven't got a shredder but my friend Karen has one.

I text her to say I'm back and she instantly invites me round for supper at the weekend. I'll take the manuscript as my plus one along with a good bottle of red.

Over in the corner the plant Karen gave me is slowly dying. Guilty of neglect, I give it water and hope for the best. What more can I do?

It's not strictly necessary but I drive up to check on the house one last time. I need to collect any post and would rather hand over the keys to the agents in person. The Fiat's engine has developed an odd sort of grumbling as if protesting that it never signed up for this many miles. If I turn on the radio, I don't have to listen to its complaints.

Kate offered to come with me but I assured her I could manage alone. Besides, she's had enough time off – she needs to pick up the threads of her own life.

Early blossoms are in flower in neighbouring front gardens. In Mum's little patch the contractors I hired have certainly been busy with the strimmer; not much has survived apart from a tiny patch of celandines.

The gate groans when I open it. Pizza flyers snag the door. Although the heating's been on low, the inside air smells stale and damp. There are two bundles of condolence cards the funeral people must have sent on. Several envelopes bear the logo of utility companies. I collect it all up and leave it in various piles on the mock-mahogany radiator cover in the hallway.

Then I take a last look in each of the rooms. The whole house seems smaller now it's without furniture. I was pleased when the money from the auction raised enough to pay for a fancy new headstone for the two of them. It's big enough to include a quotation from the Christina Rossetti poem Kate read at the funeral. *"Better by far you should forget and smile than that you should remember and be sad."* Sentiments I hope Kate has also taken to heart.

It's upsetting to look out on the back garden – once Mum's pride and joy. In the sitting room there are ghostly outlines where her pictures used to hang; I notice the indentations her heavy furniture has left on the carpets. Her bedroom no longer smells of her lavender eau de cologne. Looking up, I see there's a slight brown stain on the ceiling – probably due to a slipped roof tile. I try to picture everything as it was when she was alive but in truth the house has already lost any connection with her.

A couple with a young family are buying the house. The brash young estate agent has already told me of their plans to *totally gut the place*. I expect they'll do the same to the garden – get rid of the central flower beds and put the whole lot down to grass so the kids can run around more. In any case, it's nice to think of Mum's garden ringing with the sound children's laughter along with their inevitable squabbling.

I walk down the stairs for the very last time. In the hallway, I pick up the post and take the whole lot into the kitchen. My eyes are drawn to the gaping holes like missing teeth, where various appliances used to sit. From what I've been told the wall facing me is one of several destined soon to disappear. Presumably they've taken professional advice and the house won't fall down like a pack of cards.

I spring the elastic bands holding the condolence cards together and open each in turn. Whilst I appreciate the kind thoughts behind them, it's hard not to notice how very similar they are. The most popular images are close-ups of white lilies set against an out-of-focus background. There's a frailness to these that must be deemed appropriate. On some cards the flowers are resting on cream satin as if to evoke the flower–strewn interior of a coffin. For the rest it's a tie between wintry trees and overcast, moody skies. Two of them show sunsets and one has a half-hidden sun, which may be about to come bursting through the dark clouds or could equally be about to disappear.

One card *from Jill, Malika, Jade and Linda* has a close-up of an intact dandelion seed-head on the front – the sort I remember blowing on to tell the time. A denuded stalk would seem more appropriate under the circumstances.

Near the end of the second pile I open another with lilies on. Inside I read, *Thinking of you all at this sad time, kindest regards Sadie Robinson.* It's the woman I met at the funeral. She's attached a gold sticker with her contact details. My phone's map app informs me her house is only a slight detour from my route home. On impulse, I dial the number and ask if I can pop round for a chat.

'Please start,' I say to the car out loud. 'We're on the last leg.' Quietly so it can't hear, I add, 'Well, you are anyway.' I take it back when its starts first time.

My phone map guides me to a neat bungalow in a quiet street. Sadie takes an age to come to the door. Without the headscarf, her white hair is surprisingly thick and curly. She's wearing a flower print blouse beneath a red cardigan – clothes that make her seem younger than she did at the funeral.

She invites me in. I notice her house has the same musty smell I associate with older people and wonder if it could simply be because their doors and windows aren't opened as often.

Peering over her pink-rimmed glasses, she measures two scoops of loose tea into the teapot then arranges a plate with the sort of biscuits I might serve to kids. Though I tell her I'm fine in the kitchen, she insists we go through into her front room.

The room only just accommodates an overstuffed sofa and chairs – all facing the television set. It's chilly and so she puts on an electric fire that looks like it really ought to be PAT tested. Along the mantelpiece her family edge each other aside in their various graduation and wedding clothes.

She tells me to sit and I watch her pour the tea through a strainer. I say no to the sugar cubes she drops into her own cup. 'Shouldn't really.' She gives a conspiratorial wink as she hands me a brimming cup.

Finding no clear space to put it down, I balance the tea awkwardly and say, 'So, you worked with Mum in the hospital.'

'Aye, for a good many years. We were a merry lot – at least to start with. When she were younger, your mam was always up for a lark or a bit of teasing – anything that made the work go a bit easier. Mind you, you had to be on your toes or that ward sister brought you up sharp; made you re-do it if didn't come up to scratch. Not like it is these days. None of that, what do you call it? R.S.V.P. or whatever it is they get today.'

'M.R.S.A?' I suggest though she doesn't seem to hear.

'I'm bound to say that over the years Carol lost more and more of her sparkle – things seemed to get on top of her. Course it hit her hard when your brother Kevin went and emigrated. Would any mother. And Australia were a long way away in those days.' She shakes her head. 'It got her down – that and a few other things.'

Checking my watch, I decide it's time to get to the point, 'Did Mum tell you about my dad – about his other woman?'

Her face loses its jollity. 'She told you about all that then, did she? I am surprised.'

I can't lie to her. 'No, she didn't. But I saw Dad one time – saw the two of them together; in Leeds.'

'Oh,' she says. 'That must have been a bit of a shock.'

'Yes, it was.'

'Such a shame.' She fiddles with the cover protecting the arm of her chair. 'I 'spect you know yer mam and dad met at the hospital. Harry Preece were one of the maintenance men. Nice chap he was – always whistling. It were obvious he'd taken quite a shine to Carol. I shall never forget seeing the two of them walking out together for the first time. Me and my late husband Pete had been to the pictures and there she was on his arm, filing out alongside us. She looked so happy. "You know Harry, don't you?" she says to me and there

179

was this twinkle in her eye. A twelvemonth later they were married.' She smiles at the memory. 'Must have been a bit easier for Carol to have a man about the place. By then Kevin was getting to be a bit of a handful – needed a man to correct him like they do.'

There's no point in challenging such a statement – she's of a different generation. 'My dad really loved Kevin,' I tell her. 'Treated him like one of his own.'

Sadie nods. 'Aye, yer mam said as much.' She sips her tea – slurps might be a better word. The cup clatters against the saucer as she puts it down. 'I suppose it were the money that made Harry get a job at Garrison's the ring-binder factory. My cousin Iris worked there for a bit. Very old-fashioned it were, damned noisy to boot. Old man Garrison was a tight old so-and-so, refused to change with the times. Our Iris only stuck it out for six months. They went bust a few years after that.'

I zone out for a while as she goes into more detail about the failings of the factory.

'Anyroad,' she says, perhaps noticing my inattention. 'By all accounts it didn't take long for Harry to notice that Doreen Blenkinsopp…'

Sadie is a natural storyteller. As she talks, her skin seems to lose its slackness; the heavy folds hanging below her jaw line vibrate with the telling. I'd been to the Garrison's factory a couple of times for the children's Christmas parties they used to put on. All I recall is that I had to block my ears walking through the shop floor because of the noise.

Through Sadie's words I can picture Doreen amongst the sea of women operating the machines. Maybe it was the faulty mechanisms of her particular stamping machine that led to their first face-to-face encounter. Dad seldom talked about his work but I remember him mentioning that the women were on piecework – paid by the quantity they produced. Any breakdown would mean less money in their wage packets. My dad – Harry to her – must have seemed like a saviour as he walked through the machines towards Doreen, his spanners on a belt at his waist, his oilcan half-cocked in anticipation. Above the relentless noise she might yell in his ear, 'Damned thing seems to enjoy playing me up.'

I think he was good at his job, knew precisely how to reset the belt, or pressure or whatever was necessary to fix it. The Doreen of my imagination leaves him to it in order to take an opportunist toilet break. I picture her reapplying a bold red lipstick then adjusting the strands of hair she teases from the scarf tied for safety reasons around her head. It must have been against regulations for those loose curls to frame her face but she knows the foreman has a soft spot for her – or more likely a hard one.

Looking up when she gets back, Harry tells her, 'I'm nearly done.' Grin on his face, as he stands back wiping the grime from his hands. Having had a quick fag, she's sucking a mint and offers him one. Of course he takes it. 'Thanks. Don't mind if I do.'

Doreen's skirt ends just above her knees but not far enough up to make her mutton-dressed-as-lamb. As well as mint, she smells sweet and spicy from the latest squirt of the perfume she keeps in her locker.

Harry is concentrating on his work, on fine-tuning the

dials or whatever – the tiny adjustments he prides himself on. When satisfied, he yells above the din, 'That should do the trick. Try it now, love.'

Doreen smooths down the back of her skirt before she sits. Picking out a half-ring, she puts it in the slots. Holding a steel blade above it, she stamps down hard. She does this three more times to attach them to the blade then she holds the whole thing up to for his inspection. 'Working a treat,' she says leaning into his ear. 'That pedal's not nearly as stiff as it was.'

'It were common knowledge that Doreen Bradshaw had quite an eye for the men.' Sadie tells me. 'Rode a pushbike by all accounts; kept herself in shape as they say these days. Newly divorced an' all. Aye, the whole factory knew that despite her divorce she were still on the pill.'

Anxious no faulty blades would go before the hawk-eyes on Quality Control, the Doreen in my head slips off her stool and bends over to sort through the pieces in her crate. Peeking up her skirt, Harry contemplates the shadowy reaches of a backside that's about four dress sizes smaller than his wife's and a lot firmer. Instead of those grown-sturdy legs, hers are as shapely as a teenager's.

Doreen leans in for the killer line, 'I'll have to work on tonight or I won't make up my bonus.' Up close, she's perfectly positioned to notice his eyes dart to her undone top button. She might lick her lips before she says, 'Don't suppose I'll be finished here much before eight.'

Harry aims a stupid grin back at her. 'This has been a bit of a break for me. Been working on one of the pumps in the boiler room.' He wipes his forehead in anticipation. 'Heat in there's no joke – I could murder a pint meself.'

'Might see you in the Feather's later.' She says it as casually as you like. He rakes his hair back in place with a greasy hand. 'See you later then,' Doreen calls after him.

It's well after his usual knocking-off time when the pump is up and running. By rights he should go home. He knows Lottie will already be in bed reading. Carol will be settled in front of the telly – the sound turned up to fill the silence. On the top of the stove, the stew she always makes from Sunday's leftovers will have gone cold.

Harry takes his time washing, is careful to get the half-moons of grease out from under each fingernail. For good measure he wipes under his arms and around the back of his neck before drying himself off with a handful of paper towels.

He checks the mirror to be sure his hair is in place. For once he doesn't feel the weight that's been on his shoulders since the boy left home. They'd had the occasional flimsy airmail with an exotic postmark – nothing more. The lad seemed to be happy with his new life; there was no more to be done about it.

As he leaves the washroom, his tread is lighter than it's been of late. In the public bar of the Feather's he's halfway through his first pint when Doreen walks in. The regulars greet her with enthusiasm; he's proud to have such an attractive woman come and stand next to him. Voice catching in his throat, he asks, 'So – um – what you havin' then, lass?'

'Vodka and lime, please Harry.'

Doreen looks younger with her loose hair softening the sides of her face. The challenge in her eyes quickens his heart-rate. 'Cheers,' she says.

'Cheers,' he repeats – a fish on a hook. When she clinks her glass against his, the reverberations run through his fingers. In her easy smile he glimpses the new beginning he didn't know he was looking for.

Sadie lifts the teapot lid and says, 'Look at that, I haven't put enough water in. Let me make you another cup, dear.'

'No thanks. Really this is fine.'

'It's no trouble.'

'Honestly, Mrs um… Sadie.'

'Won't take me two ticks to top the pot up a bit. It's a long drive down to London, you need to keep your wits about you.'

'No, honestly, I'm happy with this, thanks. I'll probably stop for petrol and something to eat just past Leicester.' I drink the last of my chestnut-coloured tea to pacify her.

Sadie's features soften as she stares out of the window. Feeling the need to reciprocate, I tell her a little about Mum's life after they lost touch. While she listens, she smiles and then unselfconsciously begins to nibble the marshmallow topping off one of the biscuits before dunking it in her tea.

'We all missed your mam when she went,' she says. 'I left the hospital meself not long after. Got a job in a department store in Leeds.' She selects an iced biscuit with a hole in the middle.

For politeness sake, I choose a Jammy Dodger. I used to love them as a kid. Biting into it, the jam sticks to my teeth. With my mouth half-full, I finally get to the point – the reason I'm here. As casual as I can, I ask, 'Did Mum know about Doreen?'

'Well, I have to say it were common knowledge in the hospital. From what I heard the pair of 'em were none too discrete about it. Mind, I never breathed a word to yer mam about it. That's not to say she didn't find out from somebody.' She holds up a warning finger. 'Some are never happier than when they're spreading gossip.'

'So you think she knew about it?'

'Aye, I reckon she must have. Least ways it were obvious to everyone at the time she weren't happy. P'raps she guessed I knew; either way we never once spoke about it between us. I think she must have decided to carry on – make the best of a bad job for your sake.'

The tiny carriage clock on the mantelpiece chimes the half hour. Seconds out.

Conscious this might be my only opportunity to question someone who knew Mum when she was younger I say, 'There's one other thing I was wondering about. Did Mum ever talk to you about her first husband?'

'Not really – not to me she didn't. If anyone asked, she'd tell them he died in a car accident when she were pregnant with Kevin.' She purses her lips. 'I did notice how Carol were always quick to change the subject after that. Too painful, I suppose. Someone…' She shakes her head. 'Can't for the life of me remember who it was.' She taps her temple. 'My old brainbox isn't what it was. Anyroad, that's neither here nor there. Whoever it was told me how they'd read summat in the local paper about Stan Meakins' accident – that his car had skidded off the road and hit a brick wall. The poor soul not yet thirty and that were it for him. Some reckoned he'd been drinking. But like I say, as far as your mam were concerned the whole thing were a closed book.' She shakes her head. 'One or two swore Carol and him were heard having a massive row the night it happened but, like I said before, I don't generally pay much heed to idle gossip.'

Behind her specs, her cloudy eyes steal back to the window. She's watching the antics on the bird table just outside. Starlings have moved in en masse. They chase the smaller birds away. 'Look at them ruddy starlings. Big bullies they are.' Sadie bangs the windowpane and the birds all take off. 'Pretty birds when you look at 'em up close, but bullies all the same. I do wish they'd give the littler ones a chance. Still, you can't expect them to change their nature, I suppose.'

'You're right,' I say. 'Those things are fixed from the start.'

I finish my tea. A few minutes later I thank her and say my goodbyes.

'Mind you drive carefully,' she shouts down the path after me. That mothering instinct – once ingrained, you never lose it.

Diversion

I get in my car and head south for home. The Fiat continues to grumble, especially when I change up a gear. The radio is crackling too much so I turn it off.

It's odd to think that, all the time I was growing up, Mum might have known about Doreen. I'm grateful to Sadie for supplying me with part of the puzzle of my parents' relationship. Would Mum and I have been able to talk more freely if we'd all been able to acknowledge the existence of Dad's mistress? There may have been three of them in that marriage but the four of us were bound together in that unspoken knowledge.

Sadie has also given me a few clues to something else I've always wondered about – why Mum never talked about what happened to her first husband, Kevin's father.

I still feel guilty that I broke the promise I made to Mum. I had intended to burn all her personal things unseen and I would have done if Kate hadn't jumped the gun when she opened that needlepoint box. Okay, I'd looked through the photos she'd unearthed because I wasn't about to set light to things that are irreplaceable like that. We'd agreed to leave her personal letters unopened. There was that bundle of airmails from Kevin along with a handful of blurred photos with Stan's name on the back. For better or worse, I'd sent those on to my brother. It's only right he should have his letters back and a few keepsakes of the father he never knew. What harm can it do?

Kate and I kept one or two photos back from the bonfire in her garden where I'd burnt her letters and all the rest. I'd even consigned Mum's record of my life to the flames.

I hope Kate will treasure the needlepoint box; she can use it to store whatever she likes. I hope she chooses things that will, for her, evoke special memories.

I've allowed myself this diversion but now I'm heading home and my conscience tells me to let any remaining stones stay unturned. I've already compromised on my promise to Mum and, besides that, hadn't my ill-fated thirteenth novel taught me how impossible it is to ever find out the truth?

A few miles on, a sign tells me I'm approaching the motorway turning I need. A sudden impulse makes me pull over into a layby. A car horn protests long and hard behind me and I execute the time-honoured, two-fingered salute.

The thing that's niggling me is that local newspaper report on the accident that killed Stanley Meakins. Since all those affected are dead, what harm can possibly come from my doing a bit of digging? After all, who's to know?

Using my phone, I do a quick search for the names of the local newspaper covering that area in the 1950s. "The Beacon" and "The Evening Post" are still in print. Back copies of both papers can be viewed online. Unfortunately, and as I suspected, for the year I'm after, they haven't been scanned into any database. The third newspaper – "The Northern Herald & Advertiser" – went out of business fifty years ago.

A few more clicks and I discover a local newspaper archive with past copies viewable on microfiche. It's located up on the top floor of the city's central library. The library, together with various municipal offices, is housed in a magnificent stone building. On the screen, from the outside at least, the building looks like a royal palace. Seems it's the result of an extravagant vision by a philanthropic Victorian mill owner.

It's getting late; if I want to visit the library I'll need somewhere to stay tonight. I wish I could head back to Mum's house but that particular door is now closed and always will be from now on. I do my best not to dwell on that thought.

It's not a problem; a quick online search produces several options. This time I treat myself to a self-contained annex in the grounds of a pretty old pub – a converted outbuilding originally built to house carts according to their website. It looks lovely in the photos. The drop-pin points to somewhere on the rural outskirts of the city well away from any main roads. Perfect.

On the drive there, I notice the hedgerows are beginning to green up. A few primroses are in flower in sheltered spots on the verges. It's hard not to experience a sense of optimism when it's springtime.

Thinking back over my conversation with Sadie, I wonder if I should have told her about the time I met Doreen Blenkinsopp face to face. To this day I've never told another soul; to do so would seem like a betrayal of trust.

It was 1998. Mid-summer though you wouldn't know it from the weather. I don't know what made me seek her out a few weeks after Dad had died. His heart attack had come on out of the blue – up till then he'd always seemed perfectly fit and healthy. Not overweight; robust – I would have called him. In any case there'd been no hint of any heart condition.

At the time I was still in shock. I like to think it wasn't just idle curiosity – I needed answers. Coming to terms with my loss would be the conventional explanation and there's no denying it.

Ms Doreen Blenkinsopp – the surname and that *Ms* had stuck out from the sparse list of mourners they'd printed in the report of the funeral in the local paper; this was back when such events were seen as of local interest.

I looked her up in the telephone directory and there she was. Her address was listed beside her phone number. It was all too easy – like it was meant to be.

I had no intention of ringing ahead. Her flat was in a drab sixties block in the suburbs – not a pleasant area in those days. One Saturday morning I approached the rundown exterior from the car park. Drizzle was dampening my hair. I remember having to dodge the lines of damp washing that were festooning the walkways.

I started to worry I might have got the wrong person, even began to rehearse a lie about looking for a long-lost cousin.

Ten in the morning and she opened the door in the Co-op version of a negligee. I recognised her straight away; felt disappointed she wasn't wearing lipstick and didn't have a cigarette on the go between her fingers with their red-varnished nails.

Under the dry, blonde fringe her scrubbed face looked pretty if you ignored the smoker's lines etched around her mouth.

'My name's Charlotte Preece,' I told her. 'I'm –'

'I know who you are.' Those brown eyes didn't blink – not once.

'I wanted, want, to talk to you about my dad,' I said. 'Have you got a moment?'

She considered this for longer than I was expecting. What was I expecting? Not the upturned bicycle in the hallway, the neat and comfortable room she showed me into. The radio was tuned to a local station and Doreen turned it off before she signalled for me to sit down. I did just that. The room offered no framed photographs of the two of them together, not a trace of a man's presence in its floral coverings.

Doreen remained standing, arms folded in front; she didn't offer me tea or niceties. She said, 'So, what's brought you here?'

'I wanted – I want to ask you a few questions.'

She raised her eyebrows at that. 'Do you indeed,' she said, and then, 'What is it you want to know, exactly?'

Stupid really that I'd pictured me asking the questions; I found myself floundering. In the end I said, 'I want to know – to understand more about him.'

She made a noise that was between a scoff and a sigh. 'Harry were a good, kind man,' she said, 'and that's all you need to know.' Her hands were shaking. 'The rest ont is private, between me and him; God rest his soul.'

I thought of asking her if she truly loved him, but then thought better of it. Up until then I'd considered myself the injured party – that Mum and me were the ones with the righteous claim on him. Hers had been illegitimate. Had I come to accuse her of being the source of our family's unhappiness? Probably.

Looking into her defiant eyes, my sense of indignation dissolved. 'You're right,' I said. 'It's none of my business.' I stood up, my face burning with humiliation that I'd come at all. 'I'm sorry,' I told her.

And I retreated – headed back the way I came in, bumping into the bike in the narrowness of the hallway.

At the door she touched my shoulder. 'You know he thought the bloody world of you, don't you?' Tenderness caught in her voice. 'Else things might have turned out different.'

In Doreen's eyes I was the impediment – the one person he wouldn't or couldn't leave. She believed he loved me that much.

The two of us exchanged a look – for the briefest of moments we shared our loss. I might have hugged her had things been different. 'Thank you,' was all I said.

I remember the over-sweet smell of her perfume as she reached from behind me to open the door. Then I walked out without another word, the daylight swimming before my eyes.

Reaching the pub, I'm pleased that it's every bit as picturesque as I'd hoped. Though it's quite close to the city, when I get out of the car the air smells fresh and untainted. Daffodils nod at me from the half-barrel tubs either side of the pub entrance. An old wooden cart has been artfully placed next to one of the outbuildings. The owners must collect old farm machinery. I spot a rusting metal plough and something with a seat that looks like it might have been used in haymaking. It feels like I've stepped inside a Constable painting.

Past Times

I'm up early next morning, eager to get going. A breakfast buffet has been laid out to one side of the main bar. Someone's lit a log fire though it's currently producing more smoke than heat.

Several places have been laid ready but there's only one other diner – a bald man eating toast and marmalade. He lowers his newspaper to nod at me and we exchange a single word: 'Morning.'

In daylight, the room is sombre beneath its backbone of ancient beams. The smell of wood smoke blends with the stench of last night's stale beer. Together they interfere with the taste of my coffee. To get my money's worth I fill a bowl with muesli and a few stewed prunes and top it with plain yoghurt. I give the rest of the spread a miss though I pocket an apple for later.

Whilst I'm eating, a family makes a noisy entrance. The parents descend on the buffet with enthusiasm while the kids remain preoccupied with their colourful tablets. They sulk when the dad tells them to turn down the tinny music we can all hear. Once they've chosen what they want, the four of them sit down to eat together but no one speaks. It's not long before the parents are consulting their phones.

Outside, the air is fresher but there's a real chill to the morning. The car starts acting up again. On my fourth attempt, the engine finally catches. I make yet another resolution to take the Fiat to a garage once I'm back in London. With its MOT due in a month's time, this could easily be its last long journey – its swan song.

The narrow lanes are tricky; there seems to be a tractor or horse around every bend. Even turned up to the max, the heater is making little impact on the inside temperature. A low-lying mist is reducing visibility. I turn on the headlights. I have to intermittently wipe the inside of the windscreen to see where I'm going.

The reality of the central library doesn't disappoint – far from it. It's like walking into a place of worship. Majestic in its proportions, it stands as an illustration of the age's reverence for learning. My footsteps ring on the tiled hallway. On the stairs, I pause to admire the splendour of the domed ceiling.

It's quite a climb. Reaching the top floor, I'm a little out of breath. After the grandeur of the lower floors, the Reference Library is a bit of a disappointment. I breathe in the smell of old wood. The ceilings are a lot lower and there are no architectural flourishes to speak of. Perhaps the habit of housing servants in attics was too ingrained in the architect's vision. Hemmed in by wall-to-wall, floor-to-ceiling books, it manages to be both impressive and claustrophobic.

Behind an oversized desk, a young man is running a finger down a handwritten ledger. He could be a character out of a Dickens' novel if it weren't for the numerous piercings on his face. I can't tell if he's an employee or a researcher.

When I clear my throat, he looks up. I spot the tail of some tattooed creature protruding from his open collar. He doesn't offer to help me. Nonetheless, I explain that I'm looking for the archive of the local and regional newspapers.

Without a word he gets up and walks towards an inner doorway. I follow behind hoping I haven't misunderstood and he's simply going off to the toilet.

He stops and points to a set of labelled drawers. 'Microfiche rolls are in there.' His finger runs north to south. 'In date order.' My eyes are drawn to the stud in his tongue as he says, 'Readers are just through there. All a bit dated but they don't get used a lot these days.' Looking directly at me for the first time, he asks, 'Have you used one before?'

'Many times,' I assure him.

Frowning, he says, 'Word of warning – you need to be careful.' I wonder if this is meant as some cosmic warning before he adds, 'Particularly when you're feeding the ends through the machine. The older rolls are getting a bit fragile now.'

The air is stuffy, redolent with the musty aroma of old leather and aged paper. What few windows there are seem like an after-thought. The glass in them is dusty and hard to see through; I get the impression they're never opened in case a sudden draught might carry something irreplaceable away.

When I thank him the young man says, 'Good luck with your search,' and leaves me to it.

It's impossible to know which newspapers might have picked up the story of poor Stanley's crash. I have only a vague idea of the date. Experience has taught me the importance of approaching any research methodically. Since all three newspapers could have reported the story, I start with the most popular one – "The Beacon". My dad used to buy it every Wednesday without fail.

I get out the notepad I've brought and start to jot down the known facts. It doesn't take long to write: *Stanley Meakins. 25-29 years old. Car hits wall. Date?*

My brother Kevin is fourteen years older than me so that means he was born in 1958. Mum was only 18 at the time. Kevin's birthday is on the 16th of February – back date that around 40 weeks and, by my calculations, you get to the 14th of May as the earliest possible start date of Mum's pregnancy. It seems unlikely she had literally just got pregnant but that possibility can't be ruled out.

Opening the appropriate drawer, I select a roll that spans 1st May-31st July 1957. Unlike a computer search, with these types of readers you have to start at the beginning of the spool and work your way through issue by issue. It's tedious. Try going too quickly and you could easily miss something.

As expected, there's nothing that fits the facts in any of the May editions of the paper. I find nothing in the first part of June and then a headline pops up on the 17th:

FATAL CRASH AT
ACCIDENT BLACK SPOT.

At approximately 10:30 on Tuesday evening police were called to an accident at the junction of Mill Road with the Blackbrook turn off – a notorious accident black spot. Arriving at the scene, police discovered a blue Ford Anglia lying on its roof. It's believed the car hit a garden wall at considerable speed before overturning. It took the emergency services more than two hours to free the driver who was, tragically, pronounced dead at the scene. It's understood the victim is a local man in his late twenties. No further details have yet been released.

With no proof this driver was Stanley Meakins, I make a note of the date and rough location, the colour and make of the car and then move on.

There's nothing more in June. I move on to July. On the inside page of the 12th of July edition, a headline catches my eye:

FEARS GROW FOR MISSING
LOCAL MAN AFTER CRASH

A man is missing after his car apparently left the road, hit a wall and careered down a bank into the river below. A passing motorist, Daniel Evans, 37, spotted the upturned vehicle - thought to be a grey Morris Minor - in the river near Grassington Bridge and called the emergency services. It's believed the accident occurred on Monday evening some time between 9:30 and 11:45, the time when Mr Evan's spotted the car in the water. The emergency services were at the scene within twenty minutes but an extensive search has so far failed to locate the missing driver.

River levels remain high due to recent heavy rain and the current was especially strong at the time. A police spokesman confirmed that the missing driver is a twenty-seven-year-old local man whose identity has not yet been released.

After an initial search of the

river on Monday night, police
divers had resumed their search
as this edition went to press.

Again I note the date and location down, the make and colour
of the car and continue to the end of that roll.

The next roll spans 1st August – 31st October. Though none
of the reports specifically mention a driver in his late twenties,
I'm dismayed by the sheer number of fatal road accidents. This
was a time before airbags and other car safety features. As I
recall it wasn't compulsory to wear a seatbelt in the UK until
the early eighties

It occurs to me Stanley could have been a passenger and
not the driver so I'm about to start again when I come across
a report on the 20th of August that reads:

MISSING RIVER MAN - BODY FOUND.

Police have confirmed the body of
a young man has been discovered on
the riverbank near Kestrel Bottom
two miles downstream from Grassington Bridge. Though there has
been no official confirmation, there
is speculation that the deceased
is Mr Stanley Meakins, 28, missing
since the 11th of July when his
grey Morris Minor was apparently
involved in an accident and later

discovered upside down in the swollen river. Our reporter understands the missing man's wife and family have been informed of the development.

So there it is in black and white – at the tender age of twenty-eight Stan Meakins had drowned when his car plunged into a swollen river. How awful for Mum to have had to wait weeks for before getting this news – not knowing if her young husband was alive or dead; she must have been hoping against hope he might have somehow survived. Mum was only a teenager in 1957. Three months pregnant and now widowed before her eighteenth birthday. Imagine being told that they'd only just found his body; that her husband had lain there all that time undiscovered.

A shiver runs through me despite the room's cloying heat. What a terrible ordeal to have to live through at such a young age. It's a wonder she didn't miscarry. No surprise she couldn't bring herself to talk about it afterwards, not even to me.

All my life I've underestimated her. My eyes water at the thought of what she went through. A teenage widow, she'd had to raise her dead husband's child alone while holding down a job. Meeting my dad had brought her happiness but only for a few short years before things began to go wrong between them. Dad's long affair with Doreen could have been the cause or the symptom of their strained relationship– it's impossible to know which.

I could carry on with my search; I could try to find that report from the inquest but what would be the point?

No. My scribbled notes tell me all the facts I need to know. Let that be the end of it. I extract the spool and turn off the reader. Then I pack my things together and, on my way out, return the spool to its resting place in the archive.

I pass the young man with the piercings. He looks up. Friendlier this time, he asks, 'Did you find what you were looking for?'

'More than that,' I tell him.

Hurrying down the stairs, I'm glad to be leaving the smell of the long dead behind me. It's high time I let them all rest in peace.

On the drive home I'm hardly conscious of where I am or what I'm doing. I know the route well enough; my hands and feet do what's required without me having to consciously think about it. My mind is elsewhere.

I wouldn't say we were a happy family, but I don't think we were especially unhappy either. Perhaps Kevin was the exception – maybe he really was miserable. After he left home, it was just the three of us. Like the family in the pub this morning, we lived together but our interests rarely coincided.

Who knows why certain things stick in your mind? I remember one particular Saturday afternoon not long after Kevin left. I was sitting in what had been his place on the sofa next to Dad. Thinking about it now, I can see I must have been making a conscious effort to literally fill the gap he'd left behind.

Mum was in the same room, but she was ironing by the window while Dad and I watched the football together.

I wasn't much of a substitute; I tried to feign interest in the game but I couldn't really understand why Dad and Kevin found it so mesmerising. At school the boys were always arguing over whose team was the best. Dad explained that this match was between two rival London teams. 'A local derby,' he called it. 'That's why the fans hate each other so much.' It surprised me that living in the same city made them dislike each other more than people who lived further away. Dad looked gleeful when he said, 'There's bound to be a few punch-ups after the game.'

It puzzled me that he didn't support either team but was excited, actually sitting forward on the edge of his seat. I tried to ask him why he cared but he flapped his hand and said, 'Sush a minute, sweetheart – there's only two minutes left on the clock.'

I stayed quiet but still I couldn't understand why it mattered to him who won. 'What about your team, Dad?' I whispered. When he didn't answer I asked him again.

'They got knocked out ages ago,' Mum said. Until then I didn't think she was listening because she was busy ironing. 'That's right isn't it, Harry?' Mum sounded quite happy about this.

'Aye.' He shook his head. 'They're playing like a load of flaming fairies at the moment.'

With the match over, he got up to turn the telly off. 'But Dad,' I said, 'if your team played like fairies, they'd be fast as lightning and they could use magic to make the ball go in the net.'

I was delighted when he laughed out loud at that. Then

he stretched his arms out and said, 'May as well go and mow the ruddy lawn before it gets dark.' He ruffled my hair. 'Lottie love, you'd best go and move them dolls of yours.'

'But they're having a dollies' tea party. I've made them pretend cakes and leaf sandwiches and everything.'

We both look to Mum. 'Do what your father tells you.' She said this without looking up from whatever garment she was working on.

'But Mum–'

'No buts.' She held up her iron up like a shield. 'Do as you're told for once without that lip of yours.'

'What lip?'

She said, 'You'd best go and move them before that mower comes along else them dolls of yours won't be a pretty sight.'

Seeing my horrified face, Dad said, 'Yer mam's joking, aren't ya Carol?' When I look at Mum, I saw no trace of humour in her expression.

'Why don't I leave the bit the dolls are on,' Dad said. 'I can do it another day.'

'They've forecast rain,' Mum told him. 'There'll be a patch left in the middle twice as long as the rest ont.'

He looked from me to her. She'd planted her hands on her hips so I did the same thing.

Dad shook his head then walked towards the back door. I watched him put on his steel-capped boots – the ones he wore to stop his toes being cut off. I knew then that I'd lost the battle.

With my novelist hat on, why don't I swap to Mum's point of view – imagine things through her eyes.

It's a Saturday afternoon in September and Carol Preece has been on her feet most of the day. No wonder they're spreading out like the base of a tree – nowadays if she needs a pair of new shoes, she has to look for a size bigger and "broad fitting". Her daughter and husband are sitting down watching television and neither of them has glanced in her direction for an hour or more.

Steam from the iron is heating up her face – not something that helps the hot flushes that are plaguing her. Harry is laughing at something Lottie's said and she remembers how, at her daughter's age, on a Saturday morning she would have to wash and dress the three younger ones. Her mam would send her down to Jenkins' with a long list and she'd have to carry it all up that hill by herself. At Lottie's age, she never had a minute to herself.

She stares at the back of Harry's balding head. He might miss the lad but not like she does. He's got his mates from the factory, always has a few pints in the Feather's on a Saturday night and again Sunday lunchtimes. Comes back squiffy-eyed expecting his dinner to be on the table. Lately, he's been going out some weeknights as well. One thing's for sure, he's got the best of the deal. She's been a mother since she was eighteen and now she's approaching fifty. Thirty odd years and she sometimes wonders what's there is to look forward to.

Soundtracks

It's late when I let myself back into the flat. Looking around, it's hard to take in how different my home and the way I live is to my mum's.

Next morning, I go downstairs to collect the post that's mounted up in my absence. The box is almost full.

My neighbour Matias is doing the same thing. 'I'm going on tour next month,' he tells me. His smile could sell tooth-paste. Matias is an opera singer so I guess this is a big deal and that's why he's been looking so pleased with himself of late.

When I congratulate him, he bows his head as if he's already hearing applause. He tells me he's planning to get a tenant in to cover the mortgage on his flat while he's away. He lives in the adjoining flat and I often hear him singing when I'm out on my balcony. 'I'm going to miss being serenaded,' I tell him.

He promises to vet the prospective tenants. 'No riffraff,' he says wagging his finger and looking pleased with his use of colloquial English.

I take the post upstairs. Opening the fridge, I discover I

can't have a hot drink or cereal because the milk is well and truly off. Damn.

Leaving the post, I head off to the Co-op on the corner. Inevitably, I buy a few extras – including croissants – and spend some time at the checkout talking to Dumitra about the changeable weather we're having.

When I get back, I make coffee and munch on a croissant. I don't care about dropping crumbs on the floor because my robot cleaner is already on patrol. Outside it's turned into a fine spring day. I pour myself another cup, grab another croissant and go out onto the balcony to take in the view. Looking left to right I'm reminded of how enormous London is.

Later, I gather up the post and glance through it. Amongst the bills there's a postcard from Australia: a nighttime view of the harbour with the Sydney Opera House all lit up. Sadly, I haven't been back to Oz since my gap year. I'm vaguely contemplating a return trip as I turn the card over.

The handwriting is regular and controlled – a man's hand I would guess. It's from someone signing themselves Jerry and then in brackets: (Meakins)

Hi Charlotte,

Dad gave me your address. Going to be in London from next month and thought I might look you up, if that's ok? Would be great to meet Katie, my not-so-little cousin. Can't believe the pair of us have never set eyes on each other.

Jerry. (Your nephew!)

It's not clear whether the *pair of us* refers to him and me, or him and Kate – either way the statement is true. Being a generation removed, him and Kate might get along better than Kevin and me. What harm can it do to meet the boy? Along the bottom he's carefully printed out his contact details leaving me no wriggle room. Kate's often commented on my lack of living relatives – my somewhat stunted family tree. I prop the card up so I don't forget to respond.

I shuffle the pack and pick out a letter in a heavy vellum envelope. Straight away I recognise the handwriting as Michael's. What can he have to say to me after all this time?

He offers his condolences and then explains that he's been away and only found out about Mum's death from a mutual friend of ours. It turns out to be a good letter that manages to be both touching and poetic. Amongst other things, he describes her as a "quite a character" – an ambiguous phrase that, on Mum's behalf, I choose to take as a compliment to her. Near the end he asks me to pass on his love to Kate. This is the side of the man I fell for and I'm pleased to receive evidence that it's still there. The sign-off is rather abrupt but he's added a x next to his name.

I carry on with my chores while listening to Rag'n'Bone Man. He reaches the chorus and I turn up the volume and sing along while I sort out my neglected fridge.

My mobile vibrates against the counter. There's a text message from Duncan that simply reads,

I'm outside.

Since he's left me no choice, I buzz him in.

Like the last time he came, he's brought Ripley along. I hear the dog scrabbling up the stairs. Reaching my level, Duncan looks directly at me and says, 'I rang the bell several times but you didn't answer.' It sounds like an accusation because that's what it is.

'Sorry. I couldn't hear you,' I tell him. 'The music's too loud.' My playlist has moved on to Dua Lipa; the volume is still cranked up, neatly proving my point. Ripley is wide-eyed with alarm at Dua's "New Rules".

When I turn down the music, the dog gives a loud and very pointed sigh of relief. Taking a step backward, I'm careful to keep him at arm's length – Duncan that is, not the dog.

Ripley's enthusiastic welcome is harder to resist. His tail continues to thump the floor in time to the beat. I reach out and stroke his head and he shuts his eyes in a show of contentment.

Duncan looks as good as ever, dammit. He has a navy blue jumper slung over his shoulders and his shirtsleeves are rolled up a few turns. That stubbly beard is possibly a little longer than it was. He's always been able to carry off the casual elegance thing.

I stop stroking Ripley and the dog sinks to the floor and rests his head on his front paw though his eyes remain on me.

'So,' Duncan says, 'how have you been?' Like his dog, he narrows his eyes at me. To both I seem to be an enigma to be studied.

'Fine,' I tell him. 'Getting on with things – with life generally. Got a new book on the go so that's keeping me busy. And, before you ask, I've learnt my lesson; this one's strictly fiction.'

He grins. 'So you're back to playing the all-seeing Goddess.' He mimes someone typing. 'All that power at your tiny fingertips.'

'What can I say – it suits me better to be in control of things.'

The sun is hitting his face, lightening his hair and turning his eyes to the palest of grey greens.

I'm the first to look away. Outside I watch two pigeons strutting their stuff on my balcony, finding the crumbs from my breakfast.

'Good for you,' Duncan says. 'I'm glad to hear it.'

'And you?'

'Oh, you know – so-so.' No, I don't know and I've no right to ask. I'm relieved he has the good grace not to mention the many emails and texts he's sent me – all of them studiously ignored.

Though he remains standing, he drapes his sweater across the back of the sofa – a small claim to my territory. Ignoring the gesture, I don't invite him to sit down and I won't be offering him a coffee or anything like that. It would be dangerous for the two of us to get comfortable together – who knows where it might lead?

So there he is on his feet in front of me and I decide it's time I took a deep breath and cut to this particular chase. I say, 'How are Sarah and the boys?'

He shakes his head like he expected better. 'All of them are fine and dandy, thanks for asking.'

'As you're here, I've been meaning to ask you something.'

'Go ahead.' He opens both hands – the very picture of a man with nothing to hide.

'When you showed up at the hospital were you already planning to seduce me?' He does a good impression of being shocked. Before he can answer I say, 'Please don't lie to me, Duncan.'

Looking at the floor, he shakes his head again. 'If you want the honest truth I was acting on impulse; it was a spur of the moment thing; nothing was planned as such. Your poor mum was ill and I'm very fond of her – *was* very fond of her. And I wanted to check you were okay.'

He runs a hand through his hair, rakes it back from his face to make unblinking eye contact. 'To be fully and completely frank, at the back of my mind I may have thought there was a possibility we might – well you know…' Both hands go up again – this time in appeal.

'I see.'

'As we're being honest with each other, Lottie, perhaps you should admit that you more or less instigated what happened – you kissed me first as I recall.' He raises a hand before I can protest. 'Don't get me wrong,' he says, 'I was a more than willing participant, but I didn't do the seducing, if you can call it that.'

'You're implying I did?'

'No, I'm only saying that what happened between us was by mutual consent.' He laughs. 'God, that makes it sound like a legal defence.'

'I'm not proud of what happened, things went too far, I'll admit. But at the end of the day, I'm not the one who's married.'

From the way he flinches, I know that hit home. 'I take your point.' The tone of his voice could cut ice.

'You caught me at a weak moment and –'

'Hang on just a bloody second there.' I see the quick anger

in his eyes. 'That was below the belt, Lottie. It was never my intention to–'

'Maybe not, but the truth is I was single – am single – but you weren't and aren't.' My hands are shaking. 'I admit I went a little crazy – didn't stop to think things through. I thought I could somehow put right what happened before between you and me when...'

I take a deep breath. 'Anyway, at the time I was suffering from this illogical, frankly ridiculous fantasy that I could turn back the clock to when we were happy together. Stupid idea. Not remotely possible.'

He doesn't respond to that. 'I think perhaps I should be going,' he says, retrieving his jumper from the back of the sofa.

Reading his body language, Ripley stands up though he skids around on the hard floor. Duncan signals the dog to his side by snapping his fingers. A neat trick, such blind obedience.

Halfway to the stairs he stops. 'Listen,' he says. 'It's turned out to be a lovely day out there; why don't you come for a walk with me – with us?' He looks at the dog as if the animal's sad looking eyes ought to swing it. 'We came here in a cab, so he needs a good run around or he'll feel cheated – won't you, Ripper?'

The dog's ears prick forward in response to his name. That wagging tail sets up an urgent beat that demands an answer.

I'm in a quandary. We've known each other for more than half a lifetime and the truth is I've loved Duncan for pretty much all of that time. Do I want our relationship to come to an awkward end like this? Besides, what harm can come from a simple walk in the park? We'll be on neutral territory the whole time – both of us free to leave when we want to.

Is it really that simple? Playing for time, I smile at Ripley and ask, 'By the way, what breed is he? I'm pretty hopeless with dogs.'

'We think he might be some kind of Irish wolfhound cross.' Though I know it's unreasonable, that *we* really stings. Through the window a few marshmallow clouds are sailing in a deep blue sky. Tempting me.

'Dammit, why not?'

Just a Walk in the Park

It is mid afternoon on a sunny day and yet there's hardly anyone about. On the lake a solitary swan is making heart shapes with its reflection, posing for any stray photographer. Accepting the invitation, I take its photo along with the gang of ducks upending themselves as they dabble amongst the weeds.

When I show Duncan the results he smiles. Touching his arm, I say, 'Did you know they're sometimes called a *plump* of ducks?'

He laughs, his head tilted skywards. 'No, I did not know that,' he says. Following his gaze, I stare up at the inestimable space above our heads.

'See the clouds bubbling up there.' He nods at the sky. 'Cumulonimbus. On a day like today the earth heats up creating a warmer layer of air below the colder one above it. Because that layer of warm air is lighter, less dense than the one above, it becomes buoyant and rises up.'

I say, 'Wouldn't it be amazing if the same thing happened to people and we just floated up into the sky on days like this?'

Not to be ignored, Ripley keeps bringing back a slobbery stick for us to throw again and again. Duncan's efforts go considerably further than mine.

Passing a woman with a toddler and a pram, we follow the path around the lake then stop to lean on the railing that surrounds the deepest section – the dangerous part. I peer down into the water hoping to spot a few fish. It's impossible, there's too much reflection on the surface. Instead I watch how the otherwise solitary clouds in the water are inexorably drawn together.

'You know maybe you were right the first time.' Duncan isn't looking at me but staring across to the opposite shore.

'About what?'

'That it's not too late for us.' He laughs, though it's more of a snort. 'I mean it can't be, can it? Look at us; we're both still alive – not yet in our dotage.'

On the wires above our heads a flock of parakeets chatter together like outraged gossips. 'Come off it, Duncan.' I lace my voice with distain. 'Exactly who are you trying to kid?' My gaze crosses the bleached grass and comes to rest on a group of blousy chestnut trees.

His answer is silence.

I study the wet patch still lingering in the centre of a drying puddle. 'Going back – it's a pipedream. In reality it's never possible.'

A sudden gust whips at my hair and plasters it across my eyes to blind me. It's hard to pry it away from my skin. 'The fact is you're married to someone else and, what's more, you have two young boys to raise. That's a big responsibility.'

'I don't need reminding of my responsibilities to Ben and Charlie. I've always tried to be a good father and you know it.'

'All the same, they can't be left out of the equation.'

'Of course not.' He rubs at his forehead like a man in pain. 'You may not choose to believe me, but Sarah and I had already discussed getting a divorce before I came to the hospital. I have to admit things certainly haven't improved since I got back. Sarah is determined to move back to the States – she's been looking at places in Palo Alto. California may be beautiful but it's not for me. The firm she works for has offered her a big promotion, great salary, assisted move – the works. As far as she's concerned it's her dream job in a dream location near to her family. I'm the only impediment – the fly in her ointment.'

He looks directly into my eyes. 'Sarah's no fool; she could sense something had changed after we'd spent the night together. We had it out and she told me the real problem between her and me was that I'd never gotten over you and that she wasn't prepared to play second fiddle any longer – or some American idiom to that effect. And she was right about that.'

I can hardly take this in. He says, 'You said it to me and now I'm saying it back: it's always been you, no one else has ever got close. So you see, whatever happens, Sarah and I have reached the end of our particular road.'

His face drops. 'It's going to be hard on our boys. We've agreed they'll live with her, but I'll have them in the school holidays, fly out for birthdays and so on. Between us, we're determined to make it work.' He rubs his hands across his eyelids. 'Kids tend to adapt to these things given time.'

It's my turn to be angry. 'I see, so when you showed up at the hospital, you *were* planning some sort of reconciliation?'

'I told you it wasn't a thought-out thing,' he says. 'You keep talking about going back but my only concern is the future. All of us try to avoid thinking about our own mortality – we make decisions as if our lives are infinite when they're most definitely not. I'm going to be turning fifty this year and it's made me think long and hard about my future. A mediocre, unfulfilled existence just isn't good enough. Life has to be lived; our time should be enjoyed or else …' He drops his hands to his side. 'Or else it's all meaningless.'

'You may be right but –'

'Answer me this, Lottie, how can we decide what is or isn't possible if we're too timid to even try?' Raising my chin with one hand, he directs my gaze to his. I look right into those eyes so bright now from the lake and the sky.

I'm forced to look away when I tell him, 'I had an affair when we were married. Not long after my miscarriage.' I scoff at my choice of words. 'It wasn't exactly an affair; it was more of a physical thing – a ridiculous, stupid fucking impulse. Afterwards, I couldn't bear to tell you.'

The afternoon, the park, everything seems to grow still. I shut my eyes while I wait for his reaction. When I dare to check, his head is lowered and he's looking at the ground. He doesn't get angry, doesn't storm off across the park.

I can't stop myself from adding, 'It only happened a couple of times – a few more or less impromptu shags.'

'Who was it?' His voice is transformed and not in a good way. 'Was it someone I know? Was he – is he – a friend of ours?' He grows red in the face. 'It wasn't sodding Nigel for Christ's sake?'

'Of course not; give me some credit.'

'Then who?'

'Just a man I met. No one you know. It doesn't matter; he doesn't – didn't matter. I didn't really know him, didn't want to. Granted, he was good looking but I mean. Look, it was just sex.'

He frowns. 'What d'you mean *just* sex?' His eyes are bulging. 'I doubt there's any such thing as *just sex*.'

'You see this is exactly why I didn't tell you at the time. Why I couldn't tell you afterwards.'

He grabs my shoulders like he's about to shake me. 'So let me get this straight – you shagged some random bloke you hardly knew and then you took the whole thing out on me?'

'I wouldn't exactly put it quite like that –'

'And there was I thinking our problems were all to do with the miscarriage – with us not being able to have another baby.'

'It was all connected,' I say. 'Can't you see that?'

'No, I'm afraid you've lost me there.'

'We were both so miserable after the miscarriage. I mean, but it wasn't only about that. The truth is I don't know what made me sleep with him. And then afterwards I loathed myself for cheating on you. All that bickering and Kate was caught up in the middle of it. I suppose I was trying to take it out on *me* through you – if that makes any sense? I kept telling you at the time it was all my fault and it was.'

Ripley drops his stick at our feet and barks.

'You promised me there was no one else and like a bloody fool I believed you.' Duncan loosens his grip, lets his hands fall away. 'And now you come out with some fucking psycho-babble about not trusting me to forgive you.' He covers his face with his hands. 'Unbelievable!'

'That's not what I said. And by the way there was no one else, there never has been. I was the one who ruined everything. And I couldn't bear to make you more miserable by confessing and expecting you to forgive me. Infidelity is a betrayal – there's no getting round it. It's a fatal flaw in any relationship – like, I don't know, like a weak point in a pot that makes it ring hollow. There's no coming back from it. Look at my mum and dad; the last thing I wanted was for us to end up like them.'

When he grabs my shoulders again, I think he's really going to shake me this time; I almost will him to. Then he leans right into my face, his forehead touching mine.

We stay like that for a long time. Then he sighs and moves his head to one side, rubs his face against my wet cheek, skin on skin.

'Listen to me, Lottie,' he says. 'I know I was upset just now but the truth is none of that stuff really matters anymore. It's ancient history. The two of us can start again. New page, new book even.'

'I don't see how – '

His grip is beginning to hurt. Then he lets go and strokes the side of my face the way you might pacify an uncertain cat. And the bloody dog is bruising our legs with some enormous stick he's now found.

'Look, I haven't exactly got a master plan,' he says; 'But I really believe you and I could be happy again if we're together.'

I'm not expecting him to kiss me and when he does his lips

are cold and warm at the same time. It ends before I'm ready. Into my hair, Duncan whispers, 'Why don't we give it another go?'

I turn away, needing air, space. More clouds have bubbled up since I last looked and I think about that vast volume of air becoming too light to stay down here at ground level.

I say, 'I'm not sure. For now let's just enjoy our walk.'

We move aside for a gaggle of teenagers. When they've passed us, he smiles. 'Whatever you say.' The dog is barking to get our attention. His new stick is more like a whole branch. After a bit of a struggle, Ripley manages to raise one end in order to drop it nearer to our feet. He may be panting but I'm sure he's also smiling. Who wouldn't be happy on a beautiful day like this?

The branch is heavy and awkward but I throw the thing as far as I can and Ripley races off after it. My hands are now covered in drool.

'Will you at least consider it?' Duncan asks. 'Because I have to say, I get the impression you're not entirely averse to the idea.'

'It depends.'

'On what?'

'On who gets to keep the dog?'

'Non-negotiable,' he says, 'Ripley's staying with me – he's always been my dog.'

'Then I suppose it's a definite maybe.'

Duncan laughs. 'That's a start.' He leans forward until our noses touch like Eskimos do it. 'Should I think of a more romantic way of framing my proposal? I remember you telling me once how I needed to work on my wooing skills.'

His lips brush against mine, the contact tentative, questioning. Unable to resist, I kiss him back and he wraps his arms around me. As our embrace becomes more passionate, Ripley whines for attention and then, growing desperate starts hitting the backs of my leg with his branch.

Later, I take Duncan's arm and say, 'For now let's just play it by ear.'

'As it happens, I'm pretty good at that,' he says.

It's possible this could be the best non-decision we've ever made.

Voyage of Discovery

I'm not used to being this happy; it seems rather indecent. Most days I go around with the smuggest of expressions on my face. At night I often lie awake listening to Duncan's steady breathing hoping this dream won't end like the last one.

Living alone had seemed like the ideal setup for a writer – everything was simple and uncomplicated. It is fair to say those two adjectives no longer apply to my life.

As far as the practical arrangements go, on the surface nothing much has changed. Duncan is currently renting Matias's flat, which means the two of us are now semi-detached, or should that be semi-attached. I consider it a rather ingenious solution to our particular conundrum though I have to concede that it's a little weird that my ex-husband is also my new neighbour and my lover. I'm careful not to refer to him as my partner – that would be too big a step right now. It might jinx things.

Keeping pets is explicitly forbidden under the terms of our leases but the neighbours have taken quite a shine to Ripley and so his presence is being tolerated – for the time being at least. Luckily, he's a quiet dog not prone to barking for no good reason but I live in fear someone will shop him to the management company and that will be it. Duncan doesn't seem too worried about it.

When we first explained our proposed new setup, it's fair to say Kate didn't jump up and down with joy. Frowning she began by saying, 'Let me get this straight,' she sounded just like her father, 'the two of you are now back together. You're actually a couple again?'

'We are,' I said feeling proud of the fact. Duncan then put his arm around my shoulder to prove the point. Kate scratched her head though I doubt it was itching. 'And Sarah's gone off to California and she's taken the boys with her?' She stopped scratching and her face grew serious. 'But the two of you aren't going to be sharing this flat because Dad will be renting the one next door instead.' Hands on hips she was ready to inject a further dose of sarcasm. 'So, much the same setup as Gwyneth Paltrow and that Brad what's-his-face?'

'Not quite,' I told her. 'For a start, we're not planning on getting married.'

Duncan shot me a look. 'Not yet anyway.'

Narrowing her eyes, Kate turned on him. 'But, and please correct me if I'm wrong here, aren't you still married to Sarah?' I felt the sharp edge in her voice.

'Technically, yes.' As he said it, Duncan's arm began to weigh heavier on my shoulder.

'Ah, so it's only a *technicality*. Silly me, I thought being married to someone was supposed to mean something more than an inconvenient legality you simply choose to ignore when it suits you.' A nice turn of phrase, I had to admit.

denying the tune has a melancholy air about it. I doubt this bodes well. I pour myself a large glass of merlot and sip it while surveying the busy city below. Though it's not as polluted as some capitals, there's a definite haze over London, made worse in fine weather.

The boys will be staying with Duncan for three weeks, which means our routine will have to change. Though they're seasoned flyers, this will be the first time they've made the journey unaccompanied by either parent. Uncharacteristically, Duncan is quite anxious about the whole thing. I've done my best to reassure him that the cabin crew will be keeping a careful eye on them. I imagine that's not the only thing he's concerned about.

Duncan is planning to collect them from the airport. He hasn't asked me to go with him and I didn't suggest it. We both feel it's best to ease them into the complexities of the situation. Better to let them get over their jetlag before springing more surprises on them.

Once they've had a chance to settle in, he'll bring them round to my place for lunch. Kate's agreed to join us. I'm to be the hostess because, apart from other considerations, my kitchen table is much bigger than Duncan's. It's not like we can eat off the piano.

The music stops abruptly. A few minutes pass before Duncan appears on his balcony with a bottle of beer in hand. The two of us are separated by a wall that comes up to shoulder height on me.

'Beautiful evening,' he says.

'It certainly is.' I raise my wine in the air and say 'Cheers.'

He raises his bottle, starts to say something but a screeching police siren drowns out most of it. When it's passed on by, I say, 'I didn't catch that.'

'I said, if you squint we could be occupants in adjacent cabins on some cruise liner looking out to sea.'

'Or that bloody irritating couple from Private Lives – you know, the Noel Coward play.'

'Ah, yes.' He gives a short laugh. 'Very flat, London.'

Six for Lunch

They're all due here in forty-five minutes and I'm nervous. My main concern is how Duncan's boys are going to react to our relationship. Over the years they've encountered me in my role as their half-sister's mum but not in the guise of their dad's new girlfriend. Can someone coming up forty-seven be described as a girlfriend? In any case, they might find it hard to make the adjustment.

The final guest we're expecting is my nephew Jerry – Kevin's eldest son. After reading his postcard, Kate was really keen to meet him. His dad certainly behaved very badly over Mum's will but I won't be visiting the sins of the father upon the son. Perhaps I should have invited him here another time but he sounded upbeat and eager to meet us on the phone and he couldn't make any of the other dates I suggested.

I'm determined to serve a home-cooked meal that we can sit down to together and enjoy like a proper family. We may not be a *proper* family but we're one of sorts.

Deciding on today's menu has been tricky. Kate won't eat anything with a face. Duncan told me not to make a fuss – that the boys would be delighted with take-out pizza since their mother has banned all unhealthy food from their diet. When I specifically asked him, Jerry declared himself not a big fan of "green stuff", or fish. I was a little shocked when he said, 'I'll eat pretty much any animal including kangaroo.'

I've made two kinds of lasagna – one with mince beef, the other with veg. Thinking of Kate, I've made a mixed salad to go with it. The wholesome smell of home cooking is beginning to fill the room.

I've laid out bowls of potato crisps and some luminously orange cheesy-puffs along with olives and a hummus dip. These will accompany our pre-lunch drinks; I consider the latter essential if we're going to get through this meal in one piece. Earlier today, I cleared away all my detritus and put a cloth on the table along with a bunch of sunflowers in a jug. The nibbles are already out though I know it's a bit too early; I hope the cheese puffs won't have lost their crunch by the time they eat them. I uncork a bottle of Montepulciano and give it chance to breathe.

It's another fine afternoon and so I slide the balcony doors all the way back. A breeze begins to billow the curtains and sunlight is casting wide stripes across the floor. Ignoring the constant din of the traffic below, with half-closed eyes you could almost be somewhere in Italy.

I hear a key turning. 'It's me,' Kate shouts up the stairs. She hugs me with only slightly less enthusiasm than normal. 'Mmm, something smells good,' she says surveying the room.

At arm's length, I tell her, 'You look nice,' because the floral summer dress she's wearing really suits her.

'Thanks,' she says. 'I like you with your hair up like that. Makes you look younger.'

Feeling self-conscious, I check in the mirror to see if my makeup has survived the steam from the oven. Over on the worktop, my phone vibrates. It's a text from Jerry explaining that he's running a bit late. Does that mean five minutes or much longer?

Feet are tramping up the stairs. One after the other, Duncan, Ben, Ripley and Charlie appear. How tanned the boys are – their hair bleached almost to white by the Californian sun. A growth spurt has made Ben all legs and arms and left him a head taller than his brother. 'Ben!' Kate scoops him up, manages to lift his dangling feet a few centimetres off the ground. She only puts him down when his protests get too loud.

'Come here you.' She hugs Charlie, twirls him around until his legs fly out. Keen to get in on the action, Ripley jumps up barking almost knocking them both to the floor. When Duncan yells 'Get down,' the dog drops onto its haunches and looks penitent.

'Hi, Lottie.' Putting an arm around my shoulders, Duncan draws me to his side. No kiss. Instead he extends his other arm to shepherd his sons towards me. 'Come and say hello to Charlotte, boys.'

They do as they're told and sing-song the words *Hello, Charlotte* like children in a classroom might. To cover our mutual embarrassment, I offer them the forbidden snacks I'm bribing them with. Before accepting, they look to their father for his approval. As soon as he nods, their hands dive straight into the cheese puffs; it's best not to think about the e-numbers they're consuming. Ben pours them both a glass of Coke and they glug it down like contraband.

'Anyone care to join me in a gin and tonic?' I ask. 'We have wine or beer if you'd rather. Well, not together obviously – that would be a bit gross.' I should stop talking.

Kate gives me a look that says she's noticed I'm acting a bit weird or it could be that I'm drinking too much lately – it's disapproving however I choose to interpret it. I feel admonished when she says, 'I'm happy with water.' She dips a carrot baton in the hummus before snapping its head off.

'Well, I'd like to join you, Lottie,' Duncan says. 'A G & T might be just the thing I need right now.' I pour two generous measures of gin over ice then add lemon slices giving less room for tonic than there ought to be. Reaching for his, Duncan whispers in my ear, 'Looks like this is going to be a very long afternoon.'

The buzzer silences everyone. 'That must be Jerry,' I announce. He's only ten minutes late after all.

'Come on up,' Kate says into the intercom. Crouching down, she turns to her brothers and says, 'Jerry is my long-lost cousin; he's come here all the way from Australia. And guess what? I've never seen him before in my whole life.'

The boys' eyes light up at this puzzle. Charlie asks, 'How did he get lost?'

'That's a very good question,' Kate says. 'Let's ask him, shall we?'

Jerry is half hidden behind an impressive bouquet of flowers, which he thrusts at me. 'Thanks for inviting me, Aunty Charlotte,' he says.

I thank him and then lay the flowers aside to give him a hug. 'Call me Lottie.' He's a big lad – dark-haired and deeply tanned. When he rakes back his curly fringe, I see he's rather handsome and not a bit like his father.

He gives Kate a bear hug and calls her cuz. She blushes. Then he shakes hands with Duncan and fist-bumps the boys in turn.

'How did you get lost?' Charlie asks.

'Misread the tube map,' Jerry says. 'Rooky mistake.' I offer him a drink and he opts for a bottle of beer. 'Back home we call this a stubby,' he tells Kate. 'No need for a glass, Char – Lottie.'

Kate takes a matching beer out of the fridge. 'Cheers,' she says clinking hers against his to seal their alliance.

I find a vase for the flowers – a sunny mix of yellow and orange tulips with freesias, lilies and roses. I snip off the ends of the stems in the sink and then plunge them into the water. 'These are gorgeous,' I tell Jerry as I place them on a side table.

'Really pretty,' Kate agrees.

The timer goes off and I extract the lasagnas and carry them one at a time to the table. I place the bottle of Montepulciano in the centre along with some sparkling water. 'Sit wherever you like,' I say.

There's a bit of a kerfuffle while everyone decides where. We naturally divide into camps – Duncan next to me, Jerry next to Kate, Charlie and Ben sit side by side sandwiched between their dad and Kate.

'Please help yourselves,' I tell them.

'I think I'd better serve the boys,' Duncan says. I take his point – the food is piping hot and potentially messy if they miss their plates.

Kate and I are the only ones who choose the veggie option.

When I offer the wine round, Duncan and I are the only takers. Kate shakes her head and Jerry says, 'I'll have another stubby, if that's okay.'

'So how long have you been in London?' Duncan asks him.

''Bout two weeks,' Jerry says piling up his plate. 'They nearly didn't let me on the plane. You know at Singie airport they take your thumbprints before they let you through – well mine just didn't show up. Same thing with the rest of my fingers.' He does the jazz-hands thing. 'They made a bit of a fuss but let me through in the end. Still, I reckon if this studying lark comes to nothing, a career in crime could be the way to go.'

Wide-eyed, the boys are lapping this up. 'This food is terrific, Lottie,' Jerry says between forkfuls. He's really shovelling it down.

The boys had been toying with theirs, but I notice Charlie's now copying Jerry's technique with the fork.

Finished, Jerry sits back and says, 'That was great, Aunty.'

'Help yourself to more,' Kate says before I can.

With the beef version all gone, he eyes the alternative with some suspicion. 'Guess I could give this a go.' He takes a forkful and declares it, 'Not bad,' before refilling his plate. Between mouthfuls he says, 'Oh, before I forget, Dad told me to thank you for the photos and stuff you sent him.'

For everyone else's benefit, I say, 'Kate and I found some old photos of Stan Meakins, Kevin's father, when we were clearing out Mum's house. There were some old airmail letters too.'

'Ah yes, Stan was your mum's first husband,' Duncan says.

With his loaded fork poised, Jerry says, 'Must say the

old bastard was quite handsome when he was younger,' then carries on eating.

Though I haven't finished, I put down my knife and fork. 'Are you saying you knew him?'

'Not exactly,' Jerry says. 'I mean – '

I jump out of my skin when the wine glass in front of me shatters. Everyone reels back from the table. Red wine is streaking the tablecloth like so much spilt blood.

We stand up and check ourselves for stray fragments and cuts. 'There could be glass in the food,' Duncan says. 'We can't eat any of it.' He examines his sons for damage. Thankfully, we all appear to be unscathed.

I gingerly pick up the shards from the wineglass and put them in the dustpan Kate produces. The plates and leftovers are soon piled up on the worktop. Without being asked, Duncan puts the cloth in the sink to soak; I'm not sure it will ever be the same.

Jerry helps me wrap the broken glass up in newspaper. With the others preoccupied, I turn to him and say, 'So you know all about Stan then.'

'Not exactly. Only met the fella a couple of times, when I was a kid,' he says. 'He lived up in Queensland, which is a fair stretch from Sydney. Besides, the old man moved around a lot. I reckon I must have been about eight or nine when he died.'

'I was under the impression Stanley crashed his car and drowned here in England.' I'm tempted to tell him how I'd read about the accident – saw a photo of his submerged car and the later report when Stan's body was discovered downstream.

Jerry frowns. 'Are we talking about the same Stan Meakins – my grandpa?'

I nod.

He says, 'Did you know he was the reason Dad decided to settle in Oz in the first place? Turned out the fella wasn't much of a father. He kept buggering off – going walkabout as we say.'

'Oh, I see.' I slump down in the nearest chair.

'Is everything alright, Mum?' Kate asks. 'I'm sure the stain will come out. Odd the way that glass shattered like that; it must have had a crack you couldn't see.'

Jerry snorts. Looking at the boys he holds both hands up and wiggles his fingers. 'Or maybe it was a poltergeist...'

'What's a poddergeist?' Charlie asks.

'A ghost that likes to play tricks on people,' Jerry tells him.

Seeing his son's wide-eyed expression, Duncan says, 'Only in stories – not in real life.'

Kate is still looking at me. I turn away from her curious eyes and ask, 'Now the drama's over, who's for pud? I don't suppose you boys like ice cream.'

'Oh yes we do,' Charlie tells me. In my freezer there's a stash of artisan ice cream from the deli round the corner, which I normally keep for a rainy day. It turns out this is the start of the monsoon season.

Consequences

On autopilot, I continue to play the hostess. After the success of the ice cream, I offer coffee. Not to the boys, of course – they've had more than enough stimulants for one day.

Grinding the beans is noisy and gives me the perfect excuse not to talk to anyone. Kate makes her own green tea. She keeps giving me curious looks while I try to concentrate on the task in hand. My thoughts keep returning to Mum and the shocking conclusion that, as far as the law is concerned, she was almost certainly a bigamist. Did she know about it? If my parents' marriage was illegal, does that make me illegitimate? Technically speaking, was I born out of wedlock?

Plastering a pleasant expression on my face, I serve the coffee while I ponder the many implications of what I've just learnt. I pass around the chocolate mints as if nothing were amiss.

The conversation continues without me. Duncan shoots me a questioning look and I do my best to disarm him with a smile.

Energised by the additives I slipped them earlier, Charlie

and Ben seem content to roll around on the floor with Ripley. It's difficult to talk through the racket they're making but, by tacit agreement, we leave them be. I'd forgotten what it's like to have young children about the house and belatedly acknowledge how hard it must be for Sarah when she's working from home. It shames me that I judged her so harshly in the past, how I let jealousy affect my attitude towards her.

'Who'd like to go to the park?' Duncan asks rubbing his hands together in anticipation. 'Yeaah!' Arms raised above their heads, the boys cheer like they've just won a battle. Picking up on their enthusiasm, Ripley's tail thumps the floor like a drum.

Kate jumps up and says, 'I'll come.'

'Wish I could join you guys,' Jerry says looking at his phone. 'Afraid I'm off. Meeting a mate.' He doesn't say who or where and we don't ask. Kate doesn't hide her disappointment.

'Well, it was great to meet you all,' Jerry says heading for the stairs.

'And you,' I say. 'You must come again before you leave – if that makes sense.'

'Sure,' he says. 'Let's keep in touch.' Does he mean it? Do I mean it? It's hard to tell if this is the beginning of our relationship or the end.

Kate and I both hug him before he leaves. 'See you later,' is his parting shot.

Seeing us all on our feet, Duncan turns to me. 'You're coming with us, right?'

'No, you go ahead,' I say. 'It'll give me a chance to clear up.'

Duncan surveys the wreckage of the meal. 'I can help you do all this later.' He tilts his head to one side. 'This is England; who knows how long this weather's going to last.'

'I'm afraid I've got a headache coming on.'

He squeezes my shoulder. 'Well, if you're sure.'

Within five minutes they're all gone. Around me the sudden silence is palpable. I'm the only one left standing and staring at the mess we've all made between us.

I'm wide-awake and lying alone in the darkness. While I appreciate the airiness of this space, tonight the ceiling seems to tower over me. I study the outline of the central light fitting above my head; from this angle it looks like a noose. I'm glad Duncan is sleeping next door and I can be alone with my thoughts, my many calculations.

When they came back from the park, I claimed to have a migraine so I could retreat to my bedroom. Talk about letting sleeping dogs lie – this one should have been heavily sedated or better still strangled at birth. But it's too late now – to quote Shakespeare: *Truth will out.*

And it's my fault, no one else's. On her deathbed, Mum had more or less begged me not to 'go ferreting around' in her private things. I'd made her a promise I would burn all her personal stuff and I'd broken it. It was clear she'd been desperate to hide something – some information contained in those drawers. I didn't pay enough attention at the time but now I see how obvious it was that she had a guilty secret and was hoping to take it with her to the grave.

I had no idea when I sent off those photos with that bundle of letters that such a small, seemingly insignificant act of consideration was actually a significant betrayal. One that just came back to bite me in the arse. Though I could see they were from Australia, I didn't read any of the letters in the bundle. I'd assumed they were from Kevin, but could Stanley have written to her confessing he was still alive?

Did he deliberately stage his own death, or could it have been a fortuitous accident? A way out that presented itself to a young man eager to escape. Either way, he must have decided to abandon Mum along with his responsibilities to his unborn son. Stanley Meakins had been pronounced dead making the not yet eighteen-year-old Carol Meakins officially a widow. Of course there was no DNA testing in those days, no definitive way of identifying a body that had been exposed to the elements and possible animal predation for several weeks.

Did Mum guess it wasn't her husband – the man they found? If it wasn't Stan, whose body was it? It could have been some poor itinerant nobody had reported missing.

There are so many questions and all the people involved have taken the answers to their grave. All except Kevin, that is. Did his father confess to him? Did Kevin ever write to Mum to inform her that Stan was still alive?

Kevin must be able to shed light on what really happened.

How should I approach such a subject? Putting on the lamp, I walk through the flat and sit down at my desk. I could email him but that hardly seems appropriate under the circumstances. There's a pad of notepaper in my desk.

I pick up my pen and begin with the usual pleasantries, giving no hint of what will follow.

Dear Kevin,

We've just had lunch with your son Jerry. What a fine young man he is – you and Marcie must be so proud of him. Kate was delighted to meet her cousin for the first time. The two of them seemed to get on like a house on fire.

Yes – that's a good transitional image with a just hint of foreboding.

Jerry mentioned your father, Stanley – his grandfather. I was surprised when he said he'd met him as a child because my understanding was that the poor man had drowned in 1957. This leads me on to the crucial question I want to ask you: when and how did you find out your father was still alive and living in Australia? From what Jerry said, I wonder whether you knew he was living there before you sailed off for Sydney. I'm asking this because Mum and he were never divorced, to my knowledge. On my mum and dad's marriage certificate, which I recently came across, she's described as a widow. She was ostensibly married to my dad at the time you left. I would be grateful if you could shed some light on all this.

How does one sign off after that? After a few minutes of indecision I go with:

All best wishes,
Lottie. xxx

Once I've sealed the letter into an envelope, I leave it propped up on the kitchen worktop ready to post. It's three o'clock in the morning. Yawning, I head off back to bed. Decision made and course of action plotted, I'm able to fall asleep at long last.

It's half-past ten when Duncan wakes me. I must have been sleeping very deeply because I didn't hear him come in. He puts a mug of tea down on the bedside table then sits on the edge of the bed as he sips at his own. 'How's the head this morning?' he asks like I'm suffering from a hangover.

Sitting up I say, 'Much better now, thanks.'

'Glad to hear it. I was worried; you seemed so unlike yourself during the meal yesterday.'

I look behind him. 'Where are the boys?'

'With Clara.' I must have looked puzzled because, with an edge to his voice, he adds, 'She's my sister? Remember? I told you they were spending the day with her?'

'Of course I remember Clara; I'm still a bit sleepy, that's all.'

'Anyway,' he says. 'She and Luke collected them an hour ago. Ripley's gone with them. They're having a picnic somewhere up on the heath.'

'Sounds like fun.'

He puts down his mug. 'I didn't know you suffered from migraines.'

'Didn't you? Well I guess you know it now.'

'Hmm,' he says. 'I was wondering if you found the boys a bit too much – I mean, I know they can be noisy and pretty demanding at times…'

I put my hand on his to stop him right there. 'My headache had nothing to do with the boys. I promise.'

'Good.' I'm pleased he looks relieved. 'Anyway,' he says. They won't be back till seven o'clock, which means we've got the whole day to ourselves. I nipped down to the deli earlier and bought some of those almond croissants you like. I thought you might like breakfast in bed.'

'That's really sweet of you, but I think I'll get up now. I need a shower for a start.'

'Then I'll leave you to it,' he says.

When I stroll into the living room, I see he's laid the breakfast things out. 'This looks great,' I say. He doesn't answer, instead he holds up my letter. 'So you have a migraine that apparently poleaxes you for hours and yet, in the middle of it, you find the energy to write to your brother, even though the two of you haven't spoken since your mum's funeral.'

'After meeting Jerry, I thought I should, you know, bury the hatchet.'

He turns the letter over as if he's about to open it. I haven't convinced him. 'I'm sorry, Lottie,' he says, 'but I know you too well and I'm afraid I don't believe a word of that.'

Instead of denying it, I snatch the letter away. 'Perhaps you should mind your own bloody business.'

'Come on, this is me you're talking to. I know when there's something troubling you. As soon as Jerry mentioned his granddad yesterday, you looked like you'd seen a ghost. You were shaking. I know you did your best to explain it away – all that stuff about a migraine. To my knowledge, you've never had one before. And then you writing to your brother in the middle of the night.'

'You don't know that,' I tell him. 'I could have written it earlier this morning for all you know.'

Like some disappointed parent, he slowly shakes his head. 'Didn't we promise we wouldn't let secrets come between us again?'

He's got me. I drop the damned letter onto the table. Slumping into a chair, I rest my head on my hands. 'Then I suppose you'd better read it.'

'Are you sure you want me to?'

'No, but you're right – we agreed. We both know how destructive secrets can be and this one...' I shake my head. 'This one is a fucking big one.'

'Wow – after that billing, I kind of hope it is.' He picks the letter up and runs a knife across the top to slit it open. As he reads it his face drops. I lay my head on my arms while I wait for him to finish it.

'Jesus!' he says, 'no wonder you were acting so strangely yesterday.'

I finally look up.

'If you want my advice,' he says, 'don't send this. Kevin may or may not answer your question truthfully. Either way, I doubt he could say anything that's going to make you feel any better. He'll have heard Stan's side of the story and from what Jerry said, the old man was hardly someone to be trusted. Your mum might not have known he was alive. Maybe she found out at some point before or after she married your dad. Maybe she didn't. The poor woman's dead now – let her rest in peace.'

I groan. 'You know you have this really annoying habit of being right.'

'Not sure anyone's accused me of that before.' He smiles at me. 'Weren't you the one who told me it was impossible to know the truth? Remember that?'

'Ah yes – the book I never could finish.'

'As you rightly pointed out at the time, everyone's account of events is biased whether they're aware of it or not.'

I hold up both hands. 'So what should I do now?'

'Nothing,' he says. 'Just let it go, Lottie. At the end of the day, who really cares whether your poor mum knew she was a bigamist or not? It's all in the past.'

He bangs the table and it makes me jump. 'Life is all about this moment – the here and now. We live in the present and, when it comes down to it, that's all we have.' I recognise the sincerity in his face. 'Let's try and live in the moment and not let things that happened in the past drag us down.'

He holds the letter out. 'You can put this in another envelope and send it off hoping Kevin will answer your question, or you can rip the damned thing up and be done with it for good.'

I take it from him and hesitate. Then I tear the whole thing into tiny pieces and throw them up in the air like confetti. 'That's my girl,' he says.

'Ah, but I could always write another letter. You wouldn't know.'

'You could.' He smiles at me. 'But I don't think you will.'

About the Author

Before becoming a writer, Jan Turk Petrie taught English in inner city London schools. She now lives in the Cotswolds area of southern England. Jan has an M.A. in Creative Writing (University of Gloucestershire) and, as well as her six published novels, she has written numerous, prize-winning short stories

As a writer, Jan is always keen to challenge herself. Her first published novels – the three volumes that make up The Eldísvík Trilogy – are Nordic noir thrillers set fifty years in the future in a Scandinavian city where the rule of law comes under threat from criminal cartels controlling the forbidden zones surrounding it.

Her fourth novel – 'Too Many Heroes' – is, by contrast, a period romantic thriller set in the early 1950s – a story of an illicit love affair that angers the mobsters controlling London's East End.

Jan's fifth novel: 'Towards the Vanishing Point' is also set primarily in the 1950s and depicts an enduring friendship between two women that is put to the test when one of them falls under the spell of a sinister charmer.

'The Truth in a Lie' is Jan's first novel with a contemporary setting. It is the story of a successful writer who has a complex and often difficult relationship with her mother and her own daughter as well as with the men in her life.

Jan is a big fan of Margaret Atwood, Kate Atkinson, Philip Roth, Kurt Vonnegut and Jennifer Egan – authors who are always prepared to take risks in their writing.

Dear reader.

I really hope you've enjoyed reading 'The Truth in a Lie.' Thank you so much for buying or borrowing it.

This book means a great deal to me. If you would like to help more readers discover it, please consider leaving a review on Amazon, Goodreads, or anywhere else readers visit. It doesn't have to be a long review – a few words will suffice.

Any book's success depends a lot on how many positive reviews it gains. If you could spare a few minutes to write one, I would be very grateful. Many thanks in advance to anyone who does.

If you would like to find out more about this book, or are interested in discovering my other novels, the link to my Amazon author page is:

https://www.amazon.com/author/janturkpetrie

Or go to my website: https://janturkpetrie.com

Twitter handle: @TurkPetrie
(Twitter profile: https://twitter.com/TurkPetrie.)

Facebook author page:
https://www.facebook.com/janturkpetrie

Contact Pintail Press via the website: https://pintailpress.com

Acknowledgements

Let me begin as always by thanking John Petrie, my wonderful husband, for reading and commenting in detail on the various drafts of 'The Truth in a Lie' His feedback was invaluable and his unfailing support and encouragement helped me to finally finish this book when we were all enduring the 'lockdown' caused by the Covid 19 pandemic. Like my protagonist, Lottie, for me writing is an escape into a world I can control.

Thanks go to the rest of my family – in particular my lovely daughters Laila and Natalie – for their unwavering love and support. Special thanks go to my delightful son-in-law, Ed, for his advice on some of the medical issues. My thanks also go to my mum, Pearl Turk, for her constant encouragement and those highly prised 'Pearls of wisdom'.

As always, the feedback and encouragement from my fellow *Catchword* writers in Cirencester proved invaluable to this project. Comments from members of the highly talented *Wild Women Writers* and the feedback from Stroud's *Little George Writers Group* was also extremely helpful.

I'd like to say a special thank you to Debbie Young and everyone in the Alliance of Independent Authors (Alli) group in Cheltenham for their impressive knowledge and sound collective advice.

Lastly, I'm once again grateful to my editor and proofreader Johnny Hudspith, and to my cover designer, Jane Dixon Smith, for their consistently excellent work.

Printed in Great Britain
by Amazon